MESQUITE MAVERICK

Center Point
Large Print

Also by Eugene Cunningham and available from Center Point Large Print:

The Ranger Way

MESQUITE MAVERICK

Eugene Cunningham

CENTER POINT LARGE PRINT
THORNDIKE, MAINE

This Center Point Large Print edition
is published in the year 2026 by arrangement with
Golden West Inc.

Copyright © 1935 Eugene Cunningham.

All rights reserved.

This book is a work of fiction. All names, characters, places, and events are either products of the author's imagination or are used fictitiously. Any resemblance to actual events or locales or persons, living or dead, is entirely coincidental.

The text of this Large Print edition is unabridged.
In other aspects, this book may vary
from the original edition.
Printed in the United States of America
on permanent paper sourced using
environmentally responsible foresting methods.
Set in 16-point Times New Roman type.

ISBN: 979-8-89164-898-2

The Library of Congress has cataloged this record
under Library of Congress Control Number: 2026933163

CHAPTER 1

"What's it like to kill a man?" Edward Friarson demanded abruptly, lifting a thin face to stare at Johnny Raff.

Johnny, sitting comfortably on the edge of the O-Dot porch with one leg updrawn and chin upon that knee, took his time about answering. The last light of the sun was red; it made the tenderfoot's face seem bloody.

"Well, I never did kill a man," Johnny told his employer, in judicial tone. "So I don't know what it's like. But if you had to do it, I suppose it would be nothing much to worry about. At least, I've known a lot of men who had notches on their hoglegs, or could have put notches on, and they didn't seem to be bothered much."

"I should think—" Friarson stared straight into the sun, dark eyes unwinking, "—that the memory of it would hound a man. You read *Macbeth*."

"I wrestled it through," Johnny admitted. "There were some parts I liked a lot. But that 'damned spot' business—that's not what I'm talking about. If you'd asked me what it's like to slink around and *murder* a man—I was talking about having to kill a man, because he's going to kill you, or because he's the kind that nothing but killing will do."

"And it wouldn't worry you, if you got into one of your periodical battles in a Mesita saloon and it ended in gunplay?" Friarson persisted, without looking at the young cowboy.

"If I was pushed into killing some of those long-haired wolves in Mesita," Johnny shrugged, "I don't think it would break up my sleep a bit."

Friarson watched the crimson rim of the sun hang for a moment, then vanish over the hazy blue tip of the peak called "Squaw," leaving the "papoose" a shapeless lump upon the mountain shoulder.

"I'm still a foreigner in this High Mesa country," he said slowly, "for all that I own this O-Dot horse ranch, own half of Lewis Talbot's store in Mesita. I've learned that you can be a taxpayer, even a prominent citizen, in a community, and still be an utter stranger."

Johnny Raff locked slim, strong arms around his doubled leg and rocked a little, while he watched that thin, sensitive face. His hazel eyes narrowed calculatingly. Very slightly, he nodded while he studied his employer. He was a shrewd young man, Johnny Raff.

Edward Friarson was thirty. He was rich, well-educated—a Yale man trained in the law. But to the end of his days, he would be "Connecticut." He could not understand that for years to come, in this savage High Mesa country, the outstanding legal light would be Judge Colt.

"We'll go to town tomorrow," Friarson said abruptly. "Lewis Talbot is having trouble with Veck and Zagin again. I'd better be on hand. Talbot is likely to do something to play into their hands."

Johnny smoked without answering. In the growing dusk, Friarson's thin, solemn face showed as a hawk-nosed silhouette, sharply outlined in profile.

"Just you and I, Johnny," Friarson went on, in the tone of one thinking aloud. "There's work for the boys. You and I will be enough."

"Maybe," Johnny grunted. "But, most likely, maybe not! Look here—you're always talking peace. You want to dodge trouble. Well, not many men will pick a row with a shotgun. If you want to be let alone in the High Mesa Country, you want to look like it'll be poison and suicide to monkey with you. If you want to get to Mesita without trouble, take the three of us. If there's just two of us, we'll be a plain invitation to any of the Mesita warriors we meet."

"We're due a showdown," Friarson interrupted. "We are doomed to have it, no matter how much I try to avoid trouble. With Veck and Zagin and the rest of the politicians. With their crooked sheriff, Monty Greathouse, and his crew of thieving, gun-packing deputies."

"We are," Johnny agreed gloomily.

But he did not speak his thoughts, which

ran to the effect that the showdown was apt to find those tough old veterans, Veck and Zagin, doing the showing, and the O-Dot men in the role of watchers. He looked again at Friarson's motionless profile.

"You're the hell of a fine fellow, Ed Friarson," he thought. "I couldn't think more of you if you were my brother. But you're too—too Connecticut, ever to fit in a hardcase country. You'll never be hard enough to buck Veck and Zagin at the old, old game of bushwhacking. A showdown's coming, all right. That's certain. And when it does, lord help the little O-Dot!"

But he kept his tone carefully level when he spoke aloud, "Veck and Zagin are sore. Sore as hell! They were getting rich, loaning money to the cowmen at the rate of ten per cent a month. Then you came into the country and bought half of Lewis Talbot's store—and started loaning money at ten per cent a year! And started paying fair prices for stock. It put a crimp in the game they'd always played. Being the kind they are, Veck and Zagin won't take that lying down. Not with all the politicos in the country backing 'em up! Including the King Pin—Zeke Martinez up at Aden. Nah! They can get away scot-free with anything they think about. And trust those two to think of plenty!"

Friarson moved his thin shoulders impatiently.

"I couldn't have done otherwise. A man lives

by his convictions, Johnny. So, when I see what seems to be the right, the decent thing to do, I do it. No matter if it's not Veck and Zagin's way, I have to do it."

"Well . . ." Johnny said resignedly. "If it has got to come, it has got to come. One thing, your outfit's two-thirds for the fight—meaning Happy Isbell and me. As for Noisy Wright—"

"Noisy . . ." Friarson said meditatively, with amusement in his voice. "I like the way this country inspects a man, then puts a fitting name to him. Noisy is well named. And they call me 'The Tenderfoot,' or 'Connecticut.' Very fitting. But I've never heard you called anything but Johnny. How is that? Why are you slighted?"

"Oh," Johnny grinned, "I've never weighed enough, or made a big noise. I drifted into the High Mesa country from Texas, along with Noisy. I was pretty young, and I looked younger. I worked all around, but everybody took me for just a kid. They still do. You have got to wear long mustaches, you know, to have Veck and Zagin and Hugh Lovess and the other Big Augers take you for a man."

He stretched and yawned, then came to his feet in a single easy, tigerish movement.

"I'm going to turn in," he drawled. "We'd better be early on the road. You going to listen to good advice? Take us all with you to Mesita?"

"Oh, I suppose so," Friarson shrugged. "It

seems a little foolish, but I'll do it. I'd rather look like a bandit captain with his bodyguard than listen to your growling. And if by any chance anything *did* happen, you'd never let me hear the last of it."

"If anything did happen," Johnny said slowly, very gravely, "you'd be lucky to be able to hear anything more than the last of it—right when it happened!"

CHAPTER 2

It was a pleasant road through the mountains in the early morning, the Rio Vaca trail to Mesita. Johnny and Friarson scared up a deer, where they rode stirrup-to-stirrup in the lead of the party. In the junipers and ash and pines, birds sang, and tawny squirrels ran from rocks to trees. Johnny whistled "The Cowboy's Lament" absently, while he watched the trail ahead.

"I'm worried about Talbot," Friarson said frowningly, after a long silence. "He doesn't realize that, no matter how lawless Veck and Zagin's tactics may be, we have to abide by the letter of the law. That's a hard thing to do, in the face of their underhand methods, but it's our only chance. One day, the Governor may be persuaded to act with a little more force than he has displayed so far. When that time comes, it will mean a great deal if no lawless action can be charged against us."

"When that time comes," Johnny agreed dryly, "all this will be so aged that nobody will remember it anyway. No—my belief is that we're due a showdown long before the Governor does anything that Zeke Martinez won't like. And when that showdown comes—"

He turned in the Texas saddle to look back at the two other O-Dot punchers, "Happy" Isbell and "Noisy" Wright. Happy was a good man, a stayer. But Noisy—Johnny knew the loud-mouthed puncher very well. As he had told Friarson the night before, they had come into the High Mesa country together from Texas. They had worked for the great Spear outfit of Hugh Lovess, the cattle king; worked for those Big Augers of Mesita's crooked political ring—Veck and Zagin, the storekeepers and traders in the county seat. And the more you knew of Noisy, Johnny reflected, the less you trusted him.

"If it does come to fighting—and it's *got* to come to that, no matter what Edward Friarson wants," he told himself, "Noisy is going to do great things—for the other side!"

They rode steadily on. Noisy and Happy came charging past to take the lead. As they vanished around a curve in the trail, Johnny looked ahead with hazel eyes narrowing. Three riders were turning an elbow in the Rio Vaca trail, coming toward them from the direction of Mesita, the county seat. Johnny started, then grinned faintly. He said two words under his breath, "Elenore Lovess!"

She was a slender girl of eighteen, with black hair under a man's Stetson; with level, dark blue eyes; a smoothly red and self-willed mouth; wearing a beaded buckskin vest over a flannel shirt, trousers of fawn colored whipcord tucked into fancy inlaid half boots. She had a pearl-handled, double-action pistol swinging handily at her left side.

She lifted her hand to Johnny, smilingly. The two burly Mexican *vaqueros* escorting her merely nodded. They were the trusted retainers of Hugh Lovess, and none reared taller than the grim, grizzled cattle king. So they bore themselves accordingly.

"Hello, Johnny Raff!" Elenore greeted the one-time rider of her father. "Hasn't anybody hung you yet? Or do you always remember to cut the brand out of the hide? Good morning, Mr. Friarson! Town?"

Friarson nodded. He and Elenore grated on each other almost as much as he and Hugh Lovess irritated each other. He rode on past, leaving Johnny Raff with leg crooked around saddlehorn, facing the heiress of that cattle empire, the Spear.

"Why do you stick with him?" she snapped at Johnny. "He'll last—well, if I weren't a perfect lady, I'd say about as long as the tissue paper cat that fought the two cast iron dogs in hell! I wish you'd come back to us, Johnny. You're an awfully nice boy, and I enjoy having you around. And you're no warrior! Let the Tenderfoot Missionary to the Mesita savages hire him some long-haired gladiators with their holsters tied down, to do his fighting. He's going to wake up one fine morning soon and find that somebody's rammed a war down his neck. *You'll* get indigestion, too, from what he's bitten off. Why, I don't believe you own a pistol, Johnny!"

Johnny, head down so that his hat brim shaded his eyes, was making a cigarette. He looked up suddenly, and his young brown face was very serious.

"Thanks for the invitation," he said dryly. "But I can be miserable enough with you on the Spear, when I'm clear across on the Rio Vaca . . . Not for *this* Texas saddle tramp any closer connection. No, sir! No, ma'am! I should know my place by now when the heiress of the Spear gallops into view. Anyhow . . .

"I like Edward Friarson—more than I ever thought I'd like any man alive. He's educated, but he's never made me feel ignorant. He taught me to read and write; I've been rolling my own since I was nine, you know. He loaned me books. Maybe he even put ambition into me—we won't know that for a while, of course. And so I'm sticking with him! I've never fought except with my fists, but if that bunch of skunks in Mesita or up at Aden hit Edward Friarson, I think I'd tie down a holster or two on my own legs!"

"Yes—and get yourself killed! Well, remember the offer!"

She was gone in her usual fashion, at a headlong gallop, with the *vaqueros* quirting to keep up. Johnny watched her vanish around another turn in the trail. And, staring after her, his brown fingers worked mechanically. He looked down at the frazzled bit of paper which had been a cigarette; moved his shoulders irritably and spurred his sorrel after Friarson.

They rode in the wake of Noisy Wright and Happy Isbell for a couple of miles. Friarson suddenly leaned a little forward to stare at the two cowboys, who were a half-mile in the lead. Johnny, who had been busied with his own thoughts, looked that way, too. Noisy was waving. He and Happy Isbell both had pulled up short. Suddenly, Noisy bent over the saddlehorn, and his horse jumped sidewise, wheeled, and started up the steep hillside along which the trail ran.

Isbell whirled his mount, too, but to ride back toward Friarson and Johnny. They saw him look back, twisting his whole body in the saddle. Then he pulled in and turned back. A bunch of men now appeared around one of the crooks of the twisting trail. They trotted up to Isbell, and he came on with them.

Johnny scowled, for in the lead he saw the pinto of Jink Kesall, who was chief deputy of that political accident, Sheriff Monty Greathouse. He wondered what skullduggery had brought Kesall out on the Rio Vaca trail with four men behind him. Noisy Wright's horse still plunged up the slope, as if nothing but the uppermost peaks of the Tortugas would do. But that was nothing significant, for Johnny knew the big-mouthed cowboy inside and out. Noisy would run like a jackrabbit at the first noise, then inquire about what made him run—and invent twenty lies to plausibly explain it.

"Friarson," Jink Kesall said grimly, when the riders stopped before Johnny and his employer, "I got a warrant to search your Rio Vaca ranch for twenty-six head of stolen horses. And you better go with us, because I've got a damn good idea we'll find them horses, and when we do, I'll be putting the cuffs on you. You've been right slick, but you ain't slick enough to fool us all the time."

"Zagin's horses, by any chance? Or Veck's?" Friarson inquired evenly. His thin face was paper white except on the cheekbones, where twin scarlet patches shone. "I think that something official is about due to collide with your bunch in Mesita, and the controlling ring in Aden, as well. I'm getting tired . . ."

"Shut your damn head!" Jink Kesall snarled at him. "Raff! You keep your paw off that Winchester, or you'll wake up in hell! Same for you, Isbell! Now, you listen to me, Friarson! You have been interfering in this country just long enough! We ain't playing with you anymore. You had your warning, and you ain't took it. All right! *Now* you're going to get something else, and you're going to lick the spoon! You get that horse turned around and come with us. It'll be Mesita jail for the bunch of you, including that Noisy Wright I saw hightailing, after we've looked over your hangout!"

"Keep your dirty paws out of my face!" Friarson said sharply.

"What do you want to monkey with him for?" a hard-faced rider behind Kesall cried furiously. Johnny Raff knew him for a bad man cowboy who had been working for the tough D-Bar outfit of Joe Downer. "The son of a dog! He's needed killing a long time and . . ."

He jumped his horse forward, teeth showing yellow and hard-set under a small black mustache; little dark eyes glaring. Johnny and Isbell both spurred to get between this Simon Jones and their white-faced, but steady-eyed, employer. Kesall whipped out a pistol and turned suddenly in the saddle. He rammed the pistol muzzle into Johnny's stomach. Heinie Eddieford, also a deputy of Greathouse, and Annear, like Jones, an ex-D-Bar rider, caught Isbell's bits and stopped him. Simon Jones lifted his pistol hand, and Friarson ducked, trying to shelter himself beyond his horse.

"God damn your souls!" Johnny Raff yelled at them. He slapped furiously at Kesall's pistol that was rammed into his stomach; unconscious, almost, of what it was other than something which held him back. Kesall was turning a little to see what Jones had done. The blow knocked the Colt from his hand. Johnny jerked up the

Winchester from its scabbard under his leg.

There was a fusillade of shots now. Jones was firing almost point-blank at Friarson. A bullet struck the horse, which jumped, and unseating Friarson, ran away. Isbell had jerked out a six-shooter and was firing at Jones, over and past Heinie Eddieford and Annear. They were getting out pistols, too. Isbell's jerking horse spoiled his aim. But the horse settled on four hoofs when Annear, pistol out now, leaned over the animal's neck and fired at no more than a foot's distance, into Isbell's body.

Johnny had drawn the Winchester. He roweled his sorrel savagely, trying to get past Kesall to shoot Jones. Isbell fell from his horse, and Jones and Heinie Eddieford, with the Mexican who made the fifth of the hostile party, whirled their horses over toward Friarson. He was trying to get up, with bloody hand at his breast. They fired at him as he was almost under their horses' hoofs. Johnny jerked down the lever of his Winchester and raised the rifle. Isbell raised himself slowly on his left elbow, aiming his pistol shakily. It roared, and Annear fell out of his saddle with a hole in his right temple. Kesall was leaning from the saddle. Johnny all but ignored him. He fired at the trio over Friarson; missed. Then Kesall was up with his recovered pistol. It roared, and Johnny felt a club-like blow upon his head . . . and nothing more.

CHAPTER 3

There was water running down his face when he opened his eyes next. He found a mahogany-colored face above his own, and he stared, wonderingly. Then he recognized Felipe Espinoso, a Mexican youth who lived on the outskirts of Mesita. But even as he scowled, trying to fit Felipe into the jumble, he remembered everything, and he scrambled to his feet with an oath and stood rocking on his high heels, glaring around him.

Friarson and his dead gelding lay twenty feet away. There was Isbell, where he had collapsed after his last deadly shot at Annear. But Annear had been picked up and put at the side of the trail. Isbell's horse, like Johnny's, had vanished.

"I met them beyond here, as they rode on toward the Rio Vaca," Felipe told Johnny. "They told me to ride fast for Mesita and to say to that *hombre malo*, Greathouse, that they had met Friarson, Isbell, and you; that Friarson had shot at them and you two had joined him, killing Annear; and that they had been forced to kill you all. Will you have more whiskey?"

Johnny took the rest of the liquor in the flask. His head ached from the ripping scalp wound, upon which Felipe had put a rag from Isbell's shirt, but he could think. He went slowly over to Friarson and bent down. Friarson had been fairly shot to pieces by that last volley. Johnny's tight mouth worked, and he swallowed noisily. Friarson's mutilated face suddenly blurred as Johnny stared down. Felipe's soft, sympathetic voice roused him. He cleared his throat and blinked. Then he went through his employer's pockets and took watch, wallet, and notebook.

The name and address of Friarson's next-of-kin, a sister ten years older than he, was in the notebook, as Johnny knew. Johnny tore a leaf from the book and, upon an envelope from the pocket of the back, he painstakingly copied with Friarson's gold pencil the sister's name, the street, and number in Hartford. Then he began his letter:

> Dear Madam:
>
> This is from a cowboy working for your brother on the Rio Vaca ranch. I am writing you about the things which I find in his pockets, because he was killed by cowardly murderers today on the road near Mesita with another cowboy, a brave man, Happy Isbell. I was put out of the fight before I could kill one as Isbell killed Annear. But Jink Kesall and Heinie Eddieford and a killer called Simon Jones, and a Mexican called the Tigre are left for me. Your brother was like an older brother to me and while I never have killed a man

> in my life, I will not be able to say that tomorrow, I hope. For I will kill every one of those I have named, who are left. It is the only way down here now because the officers are rotten. It was two deputy sheriffs that led this band of murderers. Write to Kent Biddle at Mesita for he is an honest man though a lawyer, and a friend of your brother. I will give him the things from your brother's pockets. I close with respect.

He signed his name and put the note in the envelope. He took a silver dollar from his own pocket and gave it, with the letter, to Felipe. Watch, pencil, notebook, and other odds and ends, he put in Felipe's jacket pocket.

"Mail that letter without being seen. And give these things to Judge Biddle—also without being seen. Then tell the sheriff."

"But what will you do, Juan, my friend?" Felipe cried, scowling. "You have no horse. You have no gun. And when those murdering dogs come back from raiding at Rio Vaca, if they find you yet alive . . . Ah, here comes the noisy and fleet-footed one . . ."

Noisy Wright rode slowly out of an arroyo above them. Most vividly, he reminded Johnny Raff just then of an inquisitive pronghorn approaching a waving rag. He came so cautiously, so fearfully, that his very horse seemed to walk at a stiff-legged tiptoe. But he came faster when he recognized Johnny and saw no danger in Felipe. He reined in; his loose-mouthed, good-humored face working.

"My soul!" he breathed at sight of the dead. "They—they killed poor old Happy and the Tenderfoot . . ."

Then he stiffened and shook his tow-head ominously, "They needn't think they heard the last of this! Not while Bill Wright is in the running, no sirree! If I'd guessed they were aiming to hurt you all . . ."

Johnny tapped him on the knee and motioned to the ground. Noisy gaped but mechanically, almost, he swung down. Johnny reached over and twitched the reins from his slack hand.

"I'll want your horse a while, Noisy," he said quietly. "Until I can rustle another one or get back mine those thieves took. And," he leaned suddenly toward Noisy and his left hand shot out, to pull the heavy .45 from Noisy's holster, "I'll take the loan of this cutter, too."

"Say!" Noisy cried angrily. "Say! Don't think you're going to set me afoot here! And give me back my pistol! What do you think you are, anyhow! You can't put that over on me . . ."

"Shut your head!" Johnny snarled. "You yellow dog! That outfit of murderers wouldn't have bothered us if there'd been three of us beside

Edward with something to shoot! But you took your foot in your hand, as usual! You can lie down to sleep at night and get up in the mornings, after this, remembering that your yellow streak was the cause of Edward Friarson being killed—and Happy. You've no use for a pistol—or a horse. I need 'em both, and I'm taking 'em, and I swear I'd as soon bash your face in as look at you! Hand over the holster and belt, too!"

He buckled the shell belt about his lean waist and rammed the Colt into the holster. Buckskin thongs hung from the holster toe, and while the two watched him silently, he knotted the ends around his thigh. Then he swung up on Noisy's black and grunted to Felipe. He turned the horse around and started back toward the Rio Vaca.

Ten miles back was the shortcut to the house. Johnny glanced at the hoofprints of the three horses ridden by Elenore Lovess and the two *vaqueros* and saw them turn off. But the trail of the remaining four of that "shooting posse" lay ahead on the road to the O-Dot. Johnny spurred the horse on and rode with his brown face set like streaked stone, hazel eyes narrowed and hard and bright.

He stopped the horse on a slope above the little stone house, where he was concealed by juniper and scrub pine from the view of anyone watching. There was no sign of life around the house, and he looked at the sun. Kesall's bunch had had time to ransack the house and move on to round up the horses, which were all the stock on the place at the present moment. Johnny had no doubt that they were rounding up those horses. For Friarson was known to keep his money in the store at Mesita, which Lewis Talbot operated with Friarson capital, so only the horses would have drawn Kesall here.

He rode downslope presently, with Noisy's rifle across his arm. The house was empty and every piece of the simple furniture overturned. Friarson's papers were scattered from one corner of the dirt-floored main room to the other. His trunk had been battered open and clothing thrown into a pile, with old letters and pictures. The adjoining room in which the cowboys had slept was also topsy-turvy; the warbags plundered; the cots bare of blankets.

Johnny was scowling at the confusion when he heard a horse coming toward the house. He slid to a window and saw "Tigre" Lopez, the thick-set, surly Mexican of Kesall's posse, riding up. Johnny ran across the main room to the door. He had left the black there with trailing reins, and Lopez would see it as soon as he turned the corner. He jumped outside and ran along the front wall to the corner. Lopez rounded the house, and his eyes jumped to the horse, then sideways toward Johnny, leaning against the wall.

He made a guttural, grunting sound. But he

was reaching for the pistol on his thigh at first glimpse of the hipshot horse. He was fast on the draw, too. But Johnny's Colt was in his hand. He fired twice, and Tigre Lopez toppled out of the saddle, shot between the eyes and in the body. He fired a blind shot into the ground as he fell. Johnny slid toward him, pistol ready for another shot. But Tigre Lopez was dead. Johnny scowled grimly down at him.

"Now, what'd he come back for?" he wondered. He searched the body and, finding nothing but some odds and ends from the house, shrugged, "Thought he'd maybe overlooked something, I reckon . . ."

He went out to the detached cookhouse and found Dutch oven biscuit and dried beef and canned tomatoes. He got a can for coffeemaking; got bacon and coffee and sugar. He carried the food back to the front of the house and packed it in the pockets of Noisy's saddle. He took the saddle and bridle from Tigre Lopez's horse and let the animal go. Then he rode over to the little Rio Vaca, following the gunman's trail.

The O-Dot horses had been in this neighborhood when Friarson, Noisy, Happy, and Johnny had started for the county seat before dawn. There showed, presently, the hoof-cut trail of the *caballado* where Kesall's gang had bunched them and driven them on downstream. The Rio Vaca flowed southwest, cutting through Hugh

Lovess's great home-ranch and emptying into the big Rio Frontera a couple of miles west of Lovess's rambling house.

"The nervy sons of dogs!" Johnny said after a while, toward dark, when still the trail clung to the southern bank of the Vaca. "They aim to drive those O-Dot *caballos* straight up to the Spear house, I do believe! Flaunt 'em right in Hugh Lovess's face, knowing that he will have to either wink at the stealing or start a battle. Either way, it'll be too bad for the old boy. He's managed to straddle the rail without falling off on either side, so far."

He rode on through the darkness, watching for any sign that his men had made camp. But at last he pulled in and unsaddled. Evidently, they had more lead than he had expected—might even have reached the Spear house by now. So he boiled coffee and ate and lay on his blanket afterward, to smoke and study his problem.

"By the time I tangle ropes with Kesall, Eddieford, and Simon Jones," he said to himself, "I'll likely be up to my neck with all the rest of the county . . . Monty Greathouse feels mighty tall, with the Aden ring and all Zeke Martinez's influence behind him. And that low-life half-breed, Bill Veck, will keep Greathouse on the prod. He will be able to think of plenty. But if he should miss a bet, we can trust Zagin to make up the shortage."

CHAPTER 4

The trail next morning showed plain and wide, and led straight to the Spear house. But within a mile, Johnny reined in, his hand going instinctively to the smooth black butt of Noisy's Colt, as naturally as if all his life he had ridden the Blood Trail. He lifted his hard eyes up to the mountain ash and cottonwood on the left. For one horseman's trail cut off to the south, heading into the brush; a turning made the day before, of course.

"Kesall's spreading it that we opened the ball when he stopped to talk," Johnny meditated. "I'm the only one left alive, so he'll take special pains to wipe out *my* chalk-mark. Meanwhile, if I go riding up to the Spear in his drag, which way will Hugh Lovess jump? I'm just as likely to collect a slug as a kiss, at the Spear, with Kesall's story ahead. I think I'll ramble along with this fellow."

So he turned into the scrubby timber and trailed the single horseman. Near noon, going across mountain pastures toward Mesita, he ran into a sheepherder of old Nacho Howze, the half-breed sheep king. The Mexican told him that the man he trailed was four or five hours before him, a tallish man, black of hair and eyes, with a fierce face and a small dark mustache.

"Simon Jones . . ." Johnny nodded. "Did you talk with him?"

"*Sí, señor,*" the herder nodded in his turn. "He goes for the county seat. He asked what ones I had seen. I said, none."

In the late afternoon, the trail came back into the road to Mesita. The little town huddled in the shadows of the towering Tortugas was lazily peaceful on the flat below; its low buildings of gray adobe or whitish rock seeming deserted. But as he came down nearer, Johnny could see the ant-like figures of men a-horseback in the single street.

Kent Biddle's house was on the edge of town, a big whitewashed adobe in the middle of an acre of cultivated land. Johnny rode up the driveway that led from the road to stables on the side of the house. He lifted his Stetson gravely to Miss Laura, the bachelor lawyer's sister, a courtly, gray-haired lady. He asked for the judge, and she sent him on to the stables.

Kent Biddle turned at the slow rap of the hoofbeats. He was a small man, red-faced, white-haired, with a mustache and goatee of the Kentucky fashion.

"That was a terrible business, Johnny," he greeted the young man somberly. "I have been trying all day to get a warrant for the bunch. But Salazar insists that he has no evidence on which a warrant can be issued. Simon Jones is here with word from Kesall."

"Did you really expect a warrant?" Johnny said evenly, staring over the stable roof to the mountains. "From Salazar, a justice of the peace put in by Veck and Zagin? I suppose Felipe Espinoso delivered Ed's things?"

"Yes. Felipe is a good boy. Now, Johnny, you'd best turn your horse. Go lie low somewhere for a while. Noisy Wright has charged you with theft of his horse and gun. Greathouse will arrest you on sight on those charges, if not for the murder of Annear."

"Monty Greathouse couldn't *sort* of arrest me," Johnny grunted indifferently. "Did you send out for the bodies?"

"They'll be in tonight, I think. Funeral tomorrow. I'm going to be curious about their funeral, Johnny . . . Maybe it'll strike a line between Martinez's tribe and those of us who aren't on the Martinez-Veck-Zagin-Greathouse side of the fence."

"I'll be around," Johnny said in the same indifferent voice.

"Look here, Johnny!" the old lawyer exploded, stepping forward to catch the tightening reins. "What's on your mind, boy? You aren't going down the street! Not right into Greathouse's arms! You don't know what you're doing, boy! Kesall and Eddieford and Tigre Lopez, and that's a *bad* Mexican, are due to ride in any minute!"

"Not Tigre Lopez. You see, I killed him yesterday at the O-Dot. He was going to kill me, but I beat him to it. See you tomorrow."

He lifted the reins, and Biddle let them go. But he was scowling worriedly. Johnny promptly forgot the judge. He turned off the road where it became Mesita main street. He rode up to Felipe Espinoso's adobe house and swung down before the corral. Felipe ran out of the house. He looked scared. Johnny faced him without expression. Felipe repeated what the judge had said. Johnny nodded. "I'm going to leave the horse here with you, Felipe. There's a call I want to make—at the Congress Saloon. Is Greathouse at the courthouse or where? Do you happen to know?"

"He is in the store with Veck and Zagin! They are cooking up something, Juan. Will you—will you slap leather with Jones?"

Johnny nodded and moved out of the yard. He went through other yards behind adobes, for houses and stores and saloons rubbed elbows along the main street of Mesita. He came to the back of the Congress Saloon and stood for a moment listening, and a loud, familiar voice came to him. He bent a little and looked inside. Halfway along the rough pine bar stood Noisy Wright, well on the way to being drunk, by the way he teetered on high heels. He was talking with much energy, waving his hands, the whiskey sloshing occasionally out of the tin cup in his right hand.

There was no sign of Simon Jones in the Congress, so Johnny came quietly in. The drinkers, to the tally of a dozen or so, were all listening to Noisy. Johnny's soft progress went unheeded.

". . . and what does the lowdown son of a dog do, then?" Noisy cried oratorically. "I'll tell you! He asks me to let him take my pistol a minute, and me, never thinking nothin', I hand her over. He points at me and says I got to give him my horse, or else he'll kill me same's he's downed poor old Annear and . . ."

"Oh, Noisy!" Johnny called softly. "You want to make any changes in that tale, before it gets too far out and away from you?"

The tin cup struck the warped pine-planks of the floor with a clatter as Noisy Wright turned, like all the rest in the Congress, to face Johnny Raff, who stood out from the bar some ten feet, in a position where no one was directly behind him, nor anyone could get behind him with ease.

"You know, Noisy," Johnny said in conversational drawl, almost confidential in its low, good-humored note, "I have got it figured up, what your trouble is . . . It's your memory! Now, you take the case you have been spellbinding the gentlemen here about. You have clean forgot how you saw Kesall and the rest of the sneaking murderers coming, and how you on that black horse—not yours, you remember, but an O-Dot horse belonging to Friarson—went up the mountain and dived into Muleshoe Canon just like a bighorn sheep."

He let his eyes flicker to right and left, along the tense faces of cowboys and sheepherders and freighters and miscellaneous townsmen. He had the stage, so far, with no immediate danger of interruption from his audience.

"Then, Noisy, old son," he went on, smiling slightly, "you put your head out of the canon after the murders had been done and I was coming out from under Kesall's .44 that had rammed my head. You rode down the slope—remember it now, and began to breathe out puffs of smoke and spurts of red fire? *You* wanted to get Kesall, and that other son of a dog, Simon Jones, and that thieves' pup, Eddieford, that beds down in the same hogpen with Monty Greathouse, Veck, Zeke Martinez, and Zagin. *You* wanted to take out your great big pistol and shoot all the illegitimates . . . and now . . ."

As he shook his head, his expression sorrowful rather than angry, a man walking in the door might have thought the occasion anything but the amazing and unexpected affair it was. Along the bar, a representative cross-section of Mesita County's population was stiff-faced and staring-eyed. They were witnessing two near incredible things—the complete transformation of this quick-smiling, happy-go-lucky, unimportant Texas saddle tramp into a man of composure, self-possession and steely backbone second to none in all that savage region; and they were hearing what was nothing less than an open declaration of war upon the most powerful figures, not only in Mesita, but in the capital at Aden. Not even that amazing tenderfoot, Edward Friarson, had done this. He had merely gone about his affairs in Mesita as if Mesita were Hartford, Connecticut. It was doubtful if he had ever realized what he bucked. Not so Johnny Raff. He knew, and still, under the slight disguise of talking to Noisy, he had hung killing names onto the High Mesa country's tallest ones.

"You remember it all, now?" Johnny asked the silent, gaping Noisy. "Everything comes back to you? That's fine! Now, you'll recall that the black horse I borrowed from you was an O-Dot horse, and so nobody but a representative of Friarson could lay a charge of theft in the matter? And as for the gun—here it is at my side, Noisy . . . Do you want me to keep it a while longer, or do you want to get it now? If you do come on over."

There was a Colt in an old holster that hung from the belt around Noisy Wright's waist now. Noisy glared at Johnny. His faded blue eyes wandered down to the butt of his own pistol, hanging low on Johnny's left thigh, butt to the front. His hand slowly tensed, then relaxed; tensed again into a claw.

"Ah!" said Johnny. The grin widened his thin-lipped mouth. He began to walk deliberately toward Noisy, with hands swinging loose at his side. "Noisy's going to be a leather slapper now, folks! Yessirree! Step right up and have a look. This is going to be good, and you don't want to miss it. When I count three, Noisy, that'll be the time. Drop your right hand and snatch hold of the handles; count two to yourself and haul out the hogleg; pull the hammer with the thumb joint at the same time. Then . . ."

But Noisy suddenly whirled before that set smile and the all-but-imperceptible threat of the stiffening hand that brushed Johnny's thigh. He made a squawking sound and vanished through the front door. Simon Jones got up from a chair in a dusky corner of the front end of the saloon, grinning unpleasantly. He came strolling down the room, humming tunelessly underbreath.

Johnny saw him coming and, as when he waited for Tigre Lopez to turn the corner, the thing that came from somewhere far back in his mind, that made him wonder, was the way he felt. Yesterday morning, he had never shot at a man, much less killed one. He hadn't really expected ever to kill a man. But, facing that bad Mexican, he had been like a flashing machine, with directing head as cold as ice; and with absolute lack of nerves. So it was now, facing Jones, whose record in this country alone was three salty gunfighters, and who was said to rank among the fastest and most ruthless leather slappers of the Mesita region. He was even classed with Kesall and with that lean, dark, inscrutable Spear foreman, Nathan Hayes.

"My, my!" Jones drawled, grinning. "What a long tail our pup has got—to be trimmed."

"What were you hiding in the corner about?" Johnny inquired, with a grin as mirthless as Jones's own. "Afraid somebody was going to ask about that murder on the Rio Vaca trail? Hell, man! You can't get away from me by sneaking into corners! I made a little promise, out there on the road: I promised to kill every one of you yellow dogs who were on that murder. So, *come and get it, Jones!*"

The grin was wiped from the gunman's face as by a sponge—a sponge wet with vinegar, to judge by the expression replacing that sinister, contemptuous lip curling. The smack of his two hands on the curving "hogleg" butts of Colts was like the bang of a wind-slammed door. The eye could not follow the details of his draw. It was but a blurred *whirrr* like the dart and recovery of a snake striking. He had a Colt in each hand. That was all any one of the barroom's experts could say.

Fast, lightning fast, he was! All the normal advantages in gunplay were his. But Johnny

Raff had one advantage—he had provoked it; he had jarred Simon Jones off balance with the lazy mockery of his drawl; the bitter assurance that he was going to kill this alleged killer, and that he could have no trouble in doing that. So he knew that Jones was going to draw, before Jones knew it. And he was icy cold; utterly nerveless; a killing machine and nothing else. His borrowed Colt came out in a V motion of skilled, sure gun-hand.

He took a step toward Simon Jones as he snapped the Colt up to waist level and let the hammer drop; he took another step as he thumbed back the hammer again and let it go for the second shot. With the third shot, he was all but muzzle to the Texas killer. But that first shot had done the work . . . Simon Jones had been called a leather slapper; he had died here in the Congress with a cutter in each hand and not a shot fired.

"Drop that gun!" a high, shrill, shaky voice screamed at Johnny from the street door. "Damn your soul! Drop that gun, or I'll blow you plumb in two in the middle."

"Go to hell!" Johnny Raff flipped over his shoulder at Sheriff Greathouse and the double-barreled shotgun he knew Greathouse carried.

He sprang like a cat to the top of a heavy card table; half-turned to slap a slug in Greathouse's general direction; then dived out of the open window before him. He heard the shotgun roar and felt the table tremble under his feet as he left it. Then he was outside and jerking in the air, heels up, to come down to his feet and fall flat on hands and knees. He clung to his pistol and, on general principles, flung his fifth shot toward the corner of the Congress, where Greathouse might reasonably be expected to appear at any minute with his shotgun.

The bullet bit a chunk out of an adobe brick of the building corner. Somebody on the street, to the side of that corner, yelled. But Johnny was up and running like a jackrabbit for the back of the Veck-Zagin store which, with a vacant strip of land between, was the Congress's neighbor. He made the corner and rounded it unhurt.

CHAPTER 5

He could not stop, even to reload his pistol. He raced on, past the adobes in which curious women, white and brown, were framed in windows and doors. Long before he got to Felipe Espinosa and his horse, bullets were whining his way. He dodged from one small cover to another. Felipe stood at the black's neck. He had the reins up, held at the saddlehorn. Johnny stopped to look back, then reloaded the pistol swiftly. He swung into the saddle and grinned down at Felipe:

"I slapped leather with him, all right. And I'll slap leather with Kesall and Eddieford, yet, and with that slinking coyote, Greathouse! You slide out of sight and stay put till dark. Be seeing you!"

He left the yard in a clattering rush and headed out on the road that had brought him in. He rather expected to be pursued. Greathouse would see to that! But he knew this country; knew its every arroyo and canon. So, just before dark, he turned the black into a jagged gash in the Tortugas and backtracked. He came into the road once more and bent to study its dusty surface. He *had* been chased! By ten or a dozen, judging from the trail. He grinned and looked up at the moon, then set out to return to Mesita at alternate lope and foxtrot. He met nobody until he was close to the county seat, and then he turned aside to avoid the riders he heard coming.

Keeping as much as possible to the shadows, he got to the back of Lewis Talbot's store and swung down, hand on pistol, to look about. From within the store came the drone of voices, from Talbot's living quarters at the rear of the store. The barred windows in this back wall were curtained. He could only go softly to the door and knock, chancing it that Edward Friarson's partner was not talking to anyone he should not see.

There fell a silence within. He knocked again, impatiently. Though he heard no footsteps, he did hear the creaking of the old floor. Then Talbot's husky voice challenged him, from no more than a foot away. Johnny gave his name. The bar was drawn, and Talbot's face, right hand, and Colt appeared in the crack. For ten seconds, perhaps, he stared at Johnny, then stepped back. Johnny slid warily inside, but at the sight of Kent Biddle relaxed. Behind him, Talbot rebarred the heavy door.

"Well, Johnny," Biddle said slowly, "you built yourself something of a reputation today. Also—well, I think that you've started a war. What did you do, slip the posse?"

"Never saw 'em. So I started a war? Well—yeah! I see what you mean: They've been saying that Edward and Happy were killed resisting arrest, after the three of us had killed Annear. Now, I have downed one of the posse. I was a Friarson man. So it's a lick that the Friarson side was hitting when I hit Jones . . ."

"Pre-cise-ly!" Biddle nodded gravely, squinting against the gray smoke of his cheroot. "This country will be split wide open."

"Wait till I meet Kesall and Eddieford!" Johnny said between his teeth. "They'll yowl fit to hear! I'll give 'em war!"

"You don't mean that you're going to slap those two killers in the face!" Biddle cried incredulously. "Johnny! Don't crowd your luck. You managed to kill Jones—and nobody seems to know how you managed that much. But Kesall and Eddieford are different."

Johnny looked down thoughtfully at his slender right hand; he shrugged and regarded the little Kentuckian whimsically. "Don't fool yourself, Judge, about what happened in the Congress. I'm not fooling myself, and I'm not bragging when I say that Jones never had a chance to collect me. There's more to gunplay than just being fast on the draw and being a good shot. I got Jones because I knew exactly what I was going to do, and exactly what he was going to do, and I knew what he'd do before he knew it. Why? Because he moved when I pushed him! It'll be the same with Kesall and Eddieford!"

He asked Talbot for something to eat, and

when the thick-bodied, heavy-faced storekeeper was out rummaging the shelves of the store, he looked at Biddle and jerked his head toward the door. "He's next on the list, of course," he said in a low voice. "He's a sell-out to Martinez at five cents on the dollar. But if he wants to stick it out and fight, I'm with him! And I don't mean for a day or two. It's until this county is the kind of place Edward Friarson would've loved to see it. With Veck and Zagin and Greathouse and their kind shoved back clear out of things."

Talbot came back with crackers, yellow cheese, and canned peaches. He set the supper down on a table, and Johnny ate while he talked. Talbot, he knew little about, except that Edward Friarson had believed him shrewd and honest. But as they discussed the future and he saw how, time after time, the red forehead was covered with twinkling sweat to belie the impassive expression Talbot always wore, he wondered about the Talbot backbone and belly. Could the surviving partner fight? More important—would he?

"What are you figuring on doing, Talbot?" he said at last. And there was a note in his voice which jerked Talbot's eyes to him. An unconscious assumption of perfect equality.

"I do'know . . . I just do'know . . . I got a family to think about. They're in Aden, and I was aiming to bring 'em here when we got things going better. But now—hell! That Aden ring won't stop at anything! Simon Jones came to me today and asked about my selling out. Said he had heard I was going to. I know Greathouse sent him. And I know, too, who told Greathouse to send him!"

He stared dumbly at the plastered wall ahead, flinty gray eyes narrowed. His big, hairy hand came up to wipe his forehead. "Friarson never had no kin except a widow sister. When she gets that telegram of yours, Judge, wonder what she'll do? Ask you to settle up this end of his estate? The O-Dot ain't worth a hoot to anybody that ain't in the ring, and Martinez won't offer nothing for it! Same for this place. And the money we loaned out will be damn tough to collect if some of these cattlemen know the Ring is against us. How can we foreclose when the sheriff and all the rest of the officials from here to the capital won't work, except for Martinez?"

"I asked you what you figure on doing," Johnny said evenly. "But maybe it'll be better if I tell you what I'm going to do! I am going to show the Ring that they can't commit murder, even if they've got the so-called Law in their hands, without paying for it. I have started to show 'em already. And I'll show 'em something else. You know they ran off every head of stock on the place? Our *caballado*? Well, they did! Kesall and Eddieford and Jones and Lopez sold them, and I think I know where they took 'em. They sold 'em to Ward Brothers. Christy Ward was talking to Ed Friarson last week, you know, about buying horses. He went on to the Spear and the 77. My notion is, Kesall and Eddieford drove the horses over to the 77 and sold 'em to Christy."

"But what do you think you can do about it? I might get a warrant, but there's nobody here who would serve it." Biddle scowled.

"My warrant's right here," Johnny grinned, slapping his Colt. "I'll recover the horses, or I'll shoot Christy Ward's left eye out. But that's just a beginning. The question is, what's left of the firm? Will Friarson and Talbot lie down and let the Ring walk over it? If it will, I'm done with the outfit. If it wants to fight, I'll stick! But I'll be damned if I'll stand any blow hot, blow cold, Talbot . . ."

From the front door came the muffled thunder of hammering fists. Talbot scowled as he got up. Johnny grunted at him, halting him. "It's that blame Walt Jeffries of the 77," Talbot muttered irritably. "He owes us more than anybody else, and now he wants more still. I told him to come talk to the Judge and me tonight. But I told him to come to the back, and I'd let him in. If Jeffries will come over to our side and stick with the 77's riders, we've got something to buck the ring with. I better let the fool in at the front, before he busts down the door and wakes the town. He's had some drinks, I reckon."

Johnny, standing up, scowled as he watched

the thick figure go out into the store. Then, on impulse, he made a silencing gesture and slid noiselessly past Biddle to follow Talbot.

The store was dark, except where pallid moonlight came through one barred front window at an angle, to make a long whitish stripe across the floor. Talbot, muttering to himself, was taking the bar down from the front door. Johnny slid forward until he was behind the pine counter. He crouched there, where he could look around the end. He saw the door swing open, and abruptly, the opening was jammed with men. He heard Talbot's gasp of surprise.

"None of your monkey business, Talbot!" Sheriff Greathouse's voice commanded shrilly. "I'm going to search this place and the first jiggle you make of one finger, one of these boys'll cut you off pocket high! Put them hands up! Now, turn around and walk mighty slow, back towards that light! Who's in there?"

"Uh—Biddle," Talbot said after a perceptible hesitation, as he was prodded down the store. "Yeah, Judge Biddle."

"Yeah?" someone scoffed, from the Greathouse party. "I bet! You ain't seen that little horse thief Raff, I bet! Hah, I bet you ain't! Raff, you better come out of there with your paws tickling the ceiling! We aim to tote you to the jail—one way or the other."

Johnny Raff grinned. He moved to the open

front door and peered out. There was no sign of any Greathouse man out there. He went cautiously out and around the store. Nobody there. His horse still stood drowsily with reins dragging. Johnny led him softly off to a safe distance and then went back to listen at the windows. Above the noise of furious wrangling in the rear room, he distinguished Judge Biddle's voice and Greathouse's shrill replies, with the savage tones of other men interrupting. He heard his own name several times. "You ain't pulling the wool over my eyes, Biddle," Greathouse yelled. "You and Talbot were mixed up in Jones's killing, and you know where that little illegitimate, Johnny Raff, is hiding out. Now, you're going to lead us to where he is, or you're sure as hell going to wish you had! You chew on that! You're bucking the Simon Pure Quill this time, both of you!"

CHAPTER 6

There popped into Johnny's mind the statement he had made to Judge Biddle about Talbot. "He's next!" he had told Kent Biddle, in all sincerity. Here was proof that he had foreseen the next move of Veck and Zagin, for he could see nothing that led Greathouse to honestly believe that Talbot or Biddle knew anything about his movements. He had gone straight out of town from the Congress. Greathouse knew that, for it was Greathouse's men who had chased him, and that party had not returned, so they couldn't have reported anything to Greathouse.

No, this was merely another such play as Kesall had made out on the road; a weak excuse for wiping out Friarson's partner and Friarson's lawyer. He moved swiftly and soundlessly as a wolf around the store and inside. He saw the wide shoulders of a man in the door.

"We've had enough of you two in Mesita!" Greathouse was snarling as Johnny moved like a shadow, up behind the man who blocked the doorway. "You and Talbot both, Biddle! The wonder is that you lived this long! It's a plumb wonder to me!"

"With the worst thieves and murderers in the country holding county offices, that's doubtless true," Biddle drawled calmly. "I suppose you're working yourself up, now, to the point that passes with you for amazing bravery; the point where you can order your hired shoulder-strikers to shoot two unarmed men in the back."

"Ah, give it to 'em!" snarled the wide-shouldered man in the door. His hand moved restlessly, spinning the pistol by forefinger hooked in trigger guard. "They got too much to say . . ."

"Be still," Johnny Raff admonished him and cracked him hard upon the base of the skull with his Colt barrel. "Don't move—any of you!" he snarled, as "Broadshoulders" made the noise of a beheaded chicken and flopped forward into the bedroom. "For," he grinned tightly into the strained faces turned his way, "it'll be deadly and mightily catching! Up with those dirty paws, all of you!"

Greathouse and three others gaped at Johnny Raff as he squatted, scooped up Broadshoulders's pistol, and was instantly erect with two Colt muzzles peering malignantly at them from waist level. Johnny knew the others only as hardcases he had seen, from time to time, in the past year or six months, hanging around the store of Veck and Zagin, or drinking in Mesita saloons. But identification was not so important, just now. The important thing was that none had seen fit to disobey him. Each man stood lowering, with hands overhead and weapons pointing harmlessly upward.

"Take their cutters, Judge," he said grimly to Biddle. "And don't make a motion a country boy like me wouldn't *sabe* without having to go to college, while you're collecting their playthings. You see, I'm not ab-so-lute-ly certain in my mind about you. So don't start remembering what a hell of a good citizen you have always been, and how I have been loaded up with the killing of that useless scoundrel, Annear, that Happy Isbell killed. Don't try persuading me to turn myself over to the law or any of that foolishness. I'm lone-wolfing it these days. To hell with Martinez law!"

"But that's what you ought to do, nevertheless," Biddle said energetically, when all the weapons were in a pile at Johnny's feet. "The sheriff says that you killed Tigre Lopez out at the O-Dot yesterday. Greathouse calls it a murder, but I'm thinking of Tigre's reputation and saying 'killing,' you see. He intends to charge you with the murder of Annear, of Lopez, and of Jones. You can raise hell, Raff, for a while. You can doubtless raid and strike at these official murderers and thieves, but in the end, you'll be caught."

"Nice sermon," Johnny complimented him, "but if Greathouse's going into court with that bunch of lies, what's the sense of my letting him do it? He would kill me in a minute from the back; he wouldn't give me a chance. Why shouldn't I just kill him and these others of his dirty gang and call it a day? They're no more good to anybody than so many mad coyotes, and it's not as if I minded killing 'em, Judge! I'll not mind it a bit!"

Greathouse's long face turned ghastly white. The gaunt hands over his head twitched and flexed spasmodically. With bright hazel eyes fixed steadily upon the sheriff, Johnny made a jerking move of the left hand. Broadshoulders's Colt went twirling, a yard into the air. It turned over twice and fell, slapping into his ready palm. The right-hand Colt pinwheeled similarly, but steadily Johnny eyed the lank sheriff. Greathouse licked his lips. The dirty gray shirt rose and fell with his tortured breathing.

"That—that'd be murder!" he gasped, hardly above a whisper.

"Murder? *You* talk about murder!" Johny Raff cried incredulously. "It'd be a damn good job of work for the human race, I tell you! The idea of a dirty snake like you slithering around claiming to be human! Why, damn your lowdown soul!" he cried furiously. "You look like a snake! You're built like one! You never did anything in your life that a snake wouldn't do! Kill you? It'll be a pleasure, and there's not enough like you in the country to arrest me!"

Greathouse looked piteously from face to face of his silent, fascinated henchmen. He tried to speak but only made a blubbering noise. Then he screamed at the men:

"You—you—Why don't you *do* something? You just going to stand and let that murderer kill me? What the hell do I *pay* you for?"

"Don't kill him!" Biddle cried with artistic energy. "Don't kill him, Raff, not unarmed! Let him go. He'll hang himself eventually, and you won't have his blood on your hands! He can't last—no man of his kind ever does! Some of these fellows here will kill him if nobody else does! He can't buy loyalty. He's a boot-licking cur of that thief in the capital, of Zeke Martinez! Everybody knows him for what he is. So—let him go! And let those others go, too!"

"Against the wall with you!" Johnny snapped at the prisoners. "Face to it! Hands up! Put your palms flat against the wall. Talbot! Bring me about thirty feet of nice, new rope. It's all right, Judge. I reckon I'll let 'em off this time, if they don't make any bobbles and force me to drown 'em. Talbot! Bring in about five whang-leather laces too, nice, long ones."

He watched broodingly until Talbot came back. Only once did his stony face alter, and that was when he found the quiet grin hovering under the white mustache of Judge Biddle. He winked, then, at Biddle.

Talbot, coming through the door from the store, wore a mixture of expressions upon his heavy face. Nervousness, foreboding, and sardonic amusement, all were fighting for supremacy on that battleground. He held the coil of new manila in one big hand, the bundle of whang-leather laces in the other. He looked inquiringly at Johnny Raff. Broadshoulders stirred on the floor beside Johnny's foot, just then.

Johnny kicked him emphatically. The man rolled over angrily. Johnny kicked him again with a certain dispassionate thoroughness. Broadshoulders scrambled to his feet and recoiled with an oath as he found the Colt muzzle menacing him. He stared incredulously at Greathouse and the other three in their stiff, undignified positions. Johnny snarled at him, and he joined the others.

"Now, one at a time, Talbot, you'll haul down their hands and tie 'em behind their backs with the whang-leather," Johnny drawled. "And, Talbot! Same to you as to the Judge—you're working for me, and if I don't like your work, I won't fire you—I'll fire *at* you. Tie these skunks up same as if they had four legs, instead of two!"

It was done swiftly. Johnny rammed his pistols into his waistband, and in the manila rope, four feet apart, he made five nooses. Beginning with the sheriff, he put a noose about each neck until they were a coupled procession in single file. He motioned to the storekeeper, and Talbot brought the two large sides of a pasteboard box, with twine and a blacking bottle and brush. Johnny began to print a placard, making the letters large. "Martinez," he printed. Then he stopped:

"You're an educated hairpin, Judge," he said. "How do you spell 'Monkey'? Like these here, 'M-o-n-k-e-y-s'? Fine! Thanks!"

He hung the placards, one on Greathouse's breast by a loop around the sheriff's neck where he headed the line, the other hanging down the back of Broadshoulders, who was the drag of the file. Then he marched them out through the dark store into the street.

"Straight down the middle and don't stumble, anybody! Straight to the Congress Saloon. I'll be around the edges of things, remember! First man that stops, or even hesitates, he'll bite lead! No stops till you're plumb inside the saloon, and figure, all of you, how lucky you are these loops don't run up to a cottonwood limb!"

He marched them along the darkened street, which was almost deserted at this hour, with the population either abed or in the saloons. Occasional cowboys or townsmen stopped to stare, but nobody interfered with the stalking, silent procession until it came to the lighted windows of the Congress Saloon. Johnny Raff, on the right of it, lifted his voice snarlingly. Greathouse jumped at the sound and turned in under the wooden awning. Johnny saw him bump the swinging doors and watched the others trail stiffly after.

As he watched, grinning, marking how the noises of the drinkers in the Congress stopped abruptly, there came the sound of trotting horses almost at his elbow. He whirled. There was enough light, even with the moon behind a mass of clouds, to see and to be seen.

"Who's that?" Jink Kesall's voice demanded. "By the Lord, it's him. Heinie! It's Raff! Get him!"

Johnny fired as Kesall dropped off on the far side of his horse. Then he ran backward, toward a corner of the building before which he had stood, for out of the Congress, men were coming at the behest of a long, fierce yell; out of Veck and Zagin's store beyond, as well.

From the corner, Johnny fired more or less blindly at Kesall and Heinie Eddieford, and at the crowd before the store and the saloon across the street. Somebody called to him from the back of the adobe that sheltered him and rode up behind him. A youthful and lightly-brogued voice inquired eagerly of Johnny what it was that he was doing. Other hoofbeats were behind, crowding up.

Out came the moon like a lamp, out from behind a blanket of clouds. It was a big man on a big horse who asked the question. " 'Just a poor cowboy,' " Johnny answered humorously, "and the sheriff says I have done wrong! He wants to talk to me about it."

"A sheriff! Oh, praise be! Dick Quell, oh-oh, Dick! You always wanted to shoot a sheriff, and here's the chance! Sid Oldfield! 'High Pockets' Sill! It's a cowboy that's twisted the sheriff's tail—more power to him! Come along and dust off the hoglegs of you all! It's a war for the asking!"

There was the sound of creaking saddle leather and thudding feet. Before the moon slid under the clouds again, Johnny saw that the big young man of the brogue was now but one of a four-man skirmish line that extended to the next building. And without hesitation, a ripple of fire lashed up from the ground where they had dropped.

"It's more stars than the one the county give him, that sheriff will be seeing!" the big fellow yelled. "*Yaaaiii-aah!* Give 'em hell!"

CHAPTER 7

"Come on over!" The big fellow yelled at Greathouse's crowd, which had dropped down along the other side of the street to fire. "You act like you'd liver trouble! Come on over and find out about me liver regulator. Bring the war over and put her in our pot!"

The *rap-rap-rap* of bullets hammering the adobe walls was like an echo to the roar of pistols and rifles from the enemy. Johnny was grinning tightly. The march of Greathouse and his shoulder-strikers into the Congress, where everybody could see them wearing that contemptuous legend *Martinez Monkeys* would do the sheriff's cause no good. So, inevitably, it might do the Friarson side some good. They were hard-cases who played the sheriff's game, but they would be the first to roar at Greathouse as an imitation gunfighter. They would be, also, slow to tie up again to a side whose leader was of Greathouse's kind.

He fired at the flashes of the others' weapons. But sight of the front of Veck and Zagin's store gave him an idea. He grunted to the big fellow on his left and got an answer, then left the four of them to carry on the fight while he vanished into the darkness at a trot. He got his horse from behind Talbot's and crossed the street here in the darkness, where he would not be seen. He rode behind the buildings, on the other side, until he could swing down behind Veck and Zagin's. He went up to the rear door and found it ajar. He slipped inside.

They were not warriors, the paunchy, yellow faced half breed, Bill Veck, and his equally paunchy, fishy-eyed partner. Now, in safety behind the store's thick walls, they sat in a sort of alcove in the counter which served them, as Johnny knew well from his time of working for them, as an office. He slipped along the counter, careful not to stumble over the merchandise on the floor, until he was at the end of the counter and could see Veck's thick legs sticking out from his chair. Sheriff Greathouse at that moment pronounced Johnny's name with such viciousness that Johnny grinned.

"I'll stake the little son of a dog out on an anthill!" Greathouse snarled. "I'll cut out his damn heart and . . ."

"Joost as soon as you catches him, *ja*!" Zagin grunted contemptuously. "But you don't do t'ings to Johnny till you catches him! I know you, Greathouse! *Ja*! You gets to Talbot and to Biddle and you talks, talks, like always. Better you cuts the tongue from your mouth out, *ja*! And then mebbe you don't talk so that the chance to finish Talbot and Biddle, you talks away. Bah!"

"Hel-lo!" Johnny greeted them cheerfully, rising up and sheltering himself from view of anyone outside the store by stepping sideway. "How are the scalawags tonight? Howdy, Sheriff! Something happen to your neck? Rehearsing the hanging that's bound to come ahead of your burying? Too bad it was just a rehearsal."

"You!" the three men said in a voice.

"Head of the class for all of you! Me, myself! I have no agents; buy from Professor Washoe in person. I just stopped in a minute, Veck, about some business. When Greathouse's sticky fingered bushwackers hit the O-Dot, they thought we kept stolen horses in the house. Yeah! Figured they might be in Edward Friarson's trunk, or in my warbag, and they found things in the house that might've had a horse or two inside 'em—a Comanche tobacco bag of mine, for instance. Other odds and ends . . . They took 'em along."

He rammed one Colt into the waistband of his trousers and observing how six eyes hungrily followed the movement, gestured with his right-hand pistol. He leaned across to take a cigar from Zagin's private box of imported Habanas, bit off the end, scratched a match, and blew smoke at Greathouse.

"I knew you'd want to hear about it, and they being your outfit, Veck, you'd want to pay me for what they took."

"Johnny!" Zagin said rumblingly, waggling a

thick forefinger to and fro. "Better you quits this nonsense, now. You come back to work for Bill and me. We squares it all . . . Annear and Lopez and Jones. We shows you how the money makes in Mesita. *Ja*! More! *Ja*! Hey, Bill? Mesita she needs a sheriff what will not wear for the necktie the manila lass-rope! How you like it—this?"

He leaned across to Greathouse, and with deftness surprising in so fat a man, twitched the badge from the sheriff's vest. Johnny, grinning, understood that this was, in that degree at least, an honest offer; they would really make him sheriff; white-wash all charges on the books. For Bill Veck's yellow face was hopeful, his murky eyes expectant. They were out and out scoundrels both of them—but what they said they would do, they would do, for one of their own who was a two-fisted man. But he shook his head.

"No! No, thanks! I don't want the badge, Zagin. And the reason, well, you wouldn't *sabe*, so we won't talk about it. But I appreciate the offer and it surely warms my heart. I was going to hand you a bill for a thousand dollars. Now, I'll cut that half in two. It'll cost you two just five hundred for your boys' naughtiness out at the O-Dot."

"Fife hun-dreed!" Bill Veck gasped. "Fife—hun-dreed!"

"Now, now! Careful! Take your *dale vuelta*, Bill, and hold that tongue, else the cost might climb. I said five hundred, and no draft will do.

Reach into that drawer, Bill, and fork it out. Else . . .”

“*Ja*?” Zagin breathed, staring at Johnny. “*Ja*? Else . . .”

There was something strained about him, beyond the natural tension of the situation. Johnny studied that stiffness of expression for an instant, then stepped swiftly sideways, pulling his second gun. Old Hernando, man of all work about the store, and, it was said, a paid killer of Bill Veck’s for twenty years, was at his very back, with a knife in his right hand, a pistol in his left. The wrinkled face was writhed into a malignant, triumphant grin.

Johnny shoved out the left-hand gun to menace the trio before him, while his right-hand Colt flipped around. As the muzzle dug Hernando in the belly, he fired. Apparently, the slug ranged upward to penetrate the heart. For Hernando fell forward, brushing Johnny’s shoulder as he dropped.

From the open street door a man yelled, asking what the shot was for. Johnny, looking once down at the dead killer, moved his pistols significantly. Bill Veck was half erect, so that he looked like a crouching bear, with a paw out toward a shelf under the counter beyond him. Greathouse had both clawed hands up before him, rotating as if they tried to get to the pistols at his waist, but were held away from the curving butts by some invisible wall. Only Zagin sat relaxed, with one hollow blue eye squinted against his cigar's smoke. " 'S all right!" Zagin called placidly to the inquirer. "Hernando have drop his pistol. *Ja*! Go back and kill them fellas."

"Six hundred—hurry!" Johnny snapped. "Else take what Hernando had been needing so long, and got, tonight!"

Veck reached slowly for the drawer. He opened it and a half groan was torn from him. He drew out a handful of bills and groaned again. Johnny laughed.

"Why, you damned old thief! You'll have it back by tomorrow. And think how it's going to help me and my boys across the street! All there? Fine—don't count it—just hand it over!"

He bundled the sheaf of bills into a pants pocket, then bowed mockingly to them. Veck's yellow face was distorted malignantly. In that combine, Veck worshipped the money and Zagin loved the power its influence brought them. Johnny took one long step backward. "Don't be so foolish as to follow me. I'll make a couple of false starts, you see, just to save that."

"Johnny," Zagin said almost gently, "you don't think joost once more and take the badge? No-o? I am sorry. For I like you, Johnny, *ja*! And now you fights us, and very quickly you will wish you was in hell with your back broke."

"Oh, I don't know . . . maybe not. I'll probably have to kill both of you and Greathouse, of course. I don't mind killing Bill and Greathouse, Zagin. But I do sort of hate the idea of killing you. Well! I'll put some nice flowers onto your grave and drop a tear. Maybe that'll kind of salve my feelings."

He vanished into the darkness of the store without sound.

He made none of the false starts and stops he had promised them. He went like a shadow out of the back door and swung up on his horse. He rode back across the street, well down its length. He called softly to the busy warriors, who still held in check the somewhat cautious partisans of Zeke Martinez.

They delivered one final blast of fire that smashed windows in the Congress and the stores along that side. Then they swung up and, with a wild yell, whirled their horses, and galloped out of town.

"And wither away is it, my friend?" the big young man demanded cheerfully. "You were gone the hell of a long while."

"I had to go collect for the show," Johnny grinned. "Sure! I passed the hat on the other side of the street. Six hundred—maybe a bit more. The audience didn't count it."

"Six hundred!" they all yelled.

"Yeah. From the sheriff's bosses. I bet they'll just about take it out of his pay and stealings, too!"

"Something told me you were a salty rooster! Now, I am damn sure of that same!"

"Came near being! They tried to put salt on my tail over there. Well, my name's Johnny Raff and my business is battling the whole blame country, just about. What do you fellows call yourselves?"

"Oh! My name's Ralph Naile and like Sid Oldfield and 'High Pockets' Sill, I'm from Montana. Dick Quell hails from somewhere in the south of Utah. I think he's a squawman from the Navajo country. But he's like the rest of us, his room was better than his damn company! So we all came over to see what might be done about an honest living."

"What Ralph really means," the lank, sardonic Dick Quell drawled, "is a living. He just chucked in that 'honest' part for no reason a-tall."

"Well . . . if you hairpins figure you're tough enough to travel with Mesita County's outstanding murderer—I have done three murders already this week, you see—I'd like it fine. And this won't be rustling either. We'll be fighting a war, so we will guerilla-ize the other side. And I have got a notion, that between the five of us, we'll deal 'em plenty of misery from all parts of the deck."

"Listens like money from home," Ralph Naile nodded. He looked around at the others, who had pulled in behind him, to look at Johnny in the intermittent moonlight. "You know this country and we don't. Me, I'm thinking we'll do fine!"

The others grunted. Johnny gathered up his reins. "Fine!" he said. "We'll hit for the Rio Frontera now. We'll cross tomorrow and drop down on the 77. There's a scoundrel horse-buyer there I am going to make sick and sorry he ever looked at a rustled horse. Yes, sir! When we finish talking to Christy Ward, he'll be hitting for Mesita like a man getting up off of ants. And what he'll say to some deputy sheriffs and storekeepers . . ."

They made camp in a shallow cave on the west slope of the Tortugas. As they stretched out and Johnny lighted his cigarette, he laughed suddenly. Ralph Naile stared at the amused face, illuminated by the match. "Yeah? And what would be the joke?"

"Plenty! The 77's owner had been a little on the fence. Now, he is in town. So are some of his boys. Christy Ward won't have much help against us, and Veck and Zagin in Mesita will be mighty hard men to explain to, about how I rode right out of town and right to the 77 and found the horses stolen off the O-Dot. Yes, sir! I wouldn't be surprised if, sometime by the middle of next week, we should find the 77 outfit fighting right alongside us and wondering how the hell they came to be doing it!"

"Me, I am satisfied if there's a fight, and be damned to who's fighting what," Ralph yawned. "I'm beginning to like this country!"

CHAPTER 8

The Wards were not twins, though they looked it. Christy was eight or nine years the elder and much the noisier. But Johnny Raff had a notion that Oliver was more of a "stayer," even though he appeared to let Christy do most of the managing of the firm. Johnny considered this, as the five of them forded the Rio Frontera at a lonely shallow, and jogged across 77 range toward Walt Jefferies's womanless adobe house.

Ralph Naile was whistling a jig tune. He carried his gigantic figure gracefully. Daylight discovered dudishness about him; a deep crimson neckerchief; boots with diamonds and butterflies inlaid, chrome on tan; wide carved shell belt and flapless holsters; silver plated Colt .45s with steerhead pearl grips.

Sid Oldfield looked more the rusty country storekeeper than the fighting man, until his one squinting, savage blue eye rolled around. Then the dingy, wrinkled black coat and pants he wore—one leg in, one leg out of the boots, were forgotten. He rode stiffly, bobbing as his snaky, hard gaited bay broke from hard trot to harder lope.

Dick Quell was the smallest man of the five, and so lean that he looked smaller. But there was a cat-like smoothness and speed to his smallest movement that bespoke the "athlete born," as Edward Friarson had once expressed it, finding the same quality in Johnny Raff. And even Sid Oldfield's long, wooden handled six-shooter hung no more cannily than Quell's.

"High Pockets" Sill was a fat and simple faced cowboy. Johnny sized him as a follow-the-leader type, but there was enough squareness to his chin to explain his fighting of the night before. It was laziness, rather than weakness, that made him follow the line of least effort.

"A damn good bunch," Johnny complimented himself.

He looked forward again. Once over the next ridge, they would be in plain sight of anyone at the 77 house, which sat out upon a flat with a motte of cottonwoods behind it; a desolate square adobe with corrals seemingly flung down anywhere that had been easiest.

"I have got to ramble down by myself," Johnny told the four at his elbow. "If all four of you come along, it would keep anything from happening, except, maybe, a battle. But I want you to watch me and, as soon as I round the corner of the house, slide down pretty quiet and make for the cottonwoods. I figure that my arriving that way will keep anybody from noticing you."

He left them at the crest of the last rise of land, and rode straight down to the flat, then on toward the house. From behind the adobe rose a cloud of dust. Vaguely, Johnny recalled from other visits to the 77 that there was a big horse corral on that side. A corner of his tight mouth lifted, and he looked down at Noisy Wright's six-shooter. He wondered how many of the 77 riders would be there.

There were three. Two hard faced Americans and a snaky slim Mexican *vaquero*. It was the *vaquero*, standing beside the Wards, who first noticed the fall of the black's hoofs. He turned, jerking his narrow head about wolfishly. He said something and the Wards whirled about to face the rider.

They had the same narrow, long nosed faces; the same mustard colored hair; the same greenish eyes set all too close to the nose bridge. Both were long and narrow with stoop shouldered bodies. "Fences!" Edward Friarson had called them.

Now, Friarson's word popped into Johnny's mind as he rode toward them. "You can't have cow stealing on anything more than short order scale," Friarson had said that time, "without such 'fences' to buy the stolen stock. Sometimes it's beef contractors; again, butchers; still again, ranchers who want to build up their herd cheaply. But the Wards combine all of these in the single compound noun—'cattle buyers.' "

There was a bunch of horses in the round, pole

corral. Two 77 punchers were in there with them, appearing and disappearing among the horses, in the dust wreathed confusion. Johnny pulled the black to a stop ten feet from the corral gate. He slouched negligently in the saddle, hands upon the horn, hazel eyes and brown face alike, blank of expression.

"What do you want?" Christy Ward rapped at him.

There was no uneasiness on his face, or on Oliver's. Johnny thought he understood: they had not heard of anything more than Annear's death in the road. They knew nothing of Tigre Lopez's death at the O-Dot; of Simon Jones's killing in the Congress Saloon; of the march of Sheriff Greathouse, placarded, before the men of Mesita. They saw nobody riding behind him, and they were five to his one. That explained the mere irritation Christy showed, the lack of alarm.

"Just rode by, to see if any of the O-Dot horses I missed got onto 77 range," Johnny answered in a tone almost apologetic. "They will drift over this way, under certain conditions. Those are not O-Dot horses in the corral, are they?"

Christy Ward made a disgusted clicking noise and turned his back on Johnny. Oliver, shifting a trifle where he leaned against the corral, continued to watch Johnny without sound.

The Mex' *vaquero* looked at Christy, then at

Johnny, then at Christy again. How much of it he understood was a matter to guess about. But the two 77 punchers came out of the corral. They looked with entire absence of friendliness at the O-Dot man.

"You see," Johnny said softly, "Edward Friarson being murdered by the Greathouse coyotes won't settle everything. A dead man often leaves heirs. His property is what's called an estate, Ward. It's not supposed to be walked off with by the first thief that comes along."

"You got religion or something?" Oliver Ward inquired abruptly, speaking for the first time. "Wouldn't be a bad idea, at that. Come in handy when Jink Kesall hangs you, like he says he aims to for murdering poor old Annear. Anyhow, anybody could see them brands is burned."

"Anybody . . ." Johnny meditated broodingly, aloud, "anybody . . . that's covering lots of territory, Oliver. If it won't be altogether too much trouble, would you make that 'somebody' instead of 'anybody'? Somebody with ex-act-ly the right kind of eyes, you know. Because I hate like the very hell to be left out in the cold this way. And I can't see a burned brand. Not any!"

"Tell you what I can see, though; I can see horses in that corral I branded; horses I broke. But if your eyes are going back on you, the way it seems they are, I reckon you'll have to just take my word for it that those are O-Dot horses.

And, did I tell you, I'm taking 'em back to the O-Dot?"

"What you had better take," Christy Ward turned around to say very grimly, "is your foot! Take it in your hand and bust down the timber. Jink Kesall and Simon Jones and Heinie Eddieford and Tigre Lopez, they are . . ."

". . . Split up," Johnny nodded. "Yes, sir! They are that. But just for the time being. For they'll meet on the Hell roundup! Kesall and Heinie Eddieford'll meet Lopez. Because I met up with him at the O-Dot house and he had no more sense than to slap leather with me. They'll meet up with Jones, too, because I happened to run into him in the Congress Saloon, yesterday. They're burying him, because he never would keep in this warm spell we're having. They . . ."

He turned, eyes flashing. "Stay in front of me, *hombre*!" he snarled at the *vaquero*. "Else you'll meet Lopez and Jones before the others do!"

CHAPTER 9

Christy and Oliver Ward looked even more like twins. For the tight mouths of both were gaping as they stared at Johnny. Christy was first to click teeth together and sneer.

"I bet!" he said. "And if you think for a minute I'm handing over forty head of horses I bought and paid for, because a fool kid comes trying to run a sandy . . ."

"Don't strain yourself!" Johnny counseled him. "You know . . . you're a precious pair of lousy thieves, you and Oliver! If I thought it'd do a speck of good, I'd preach you a hell of a good sermon. But it wouldn't. So I won't preach at you, I'll prophesy for you: You're about done in this whole High Mesa country. Maybe in every country this side of Jordan River, you Wards. Plumb done! You . . .

"I *told* you to stay in front of me!" he snarled at the *vaquero*, who was sliding sideway with hand on the pistol in his sash.

The Mexican gave over all pretense of innocence, now. The brown hand closed convulsively on the six-shooter butt. It flicked out of the sash.

But Johnny Raff's hand jumped from the saddlehorn to the butt of Noisy's Colt. The gun came out cocked, with a blurry snap. Johnny let the hammer drop with the side swing of it. The *vaquero* dropped without a sound, with a hole in his forehead.

There was no need for a second look at him! Johnny swung the Colt around. For there was tension in front of him. Through the four remaining men a kind of tightness seemed to run, like a cloud shadow over grass.

"You—You—" Christy Ward began. Oliver said nothing. He was leaning against the corral again, thumb hooked in his belt above his pistol. He only regarded Johnny thoughtfully. The two 77 men seemed uncertain.

"I ought to hang you two thieves to that gate bar!" Johnny told the Wards viciously. "It'd make the country a sight cleaner. Any of you feel like slapping leather with me? Any two of you? All four of you? Not that I have got any quarrel with the 77. Jefferies is not the man to knowingly mix up in horse stealing. He's got his weaknesses, but mixing into a coldblooded steal like Jink Kesall and you two Wards tried is enough to turn the stomach of anybody but skunks like you, Christy Ward, and that goes for you, Oliver! You—"

There was no sound at all. Nothing to warn him of danger at his back, as he dropped the words which would push Walt Jefferies over to the side opposite the Martinez Ring, except a sudden triumphant glint in Christy Ward's green eyes.

And Johnny hardly dared turn his head from them, to see what was behind him.

In the fraction of a second which he hesitated, there came the roar of a pistol from the house front. His hat jumped from his head. The Colt roared again and the black horse collapsed under him like something made of tissue paper, dropping with an almost human groan.

There was no time to clear his feet of tapaderoed stirrups. He was caught under the black and sprawled there, clinging to his six-shooter, the weight of the big gelding on his right thigh, the breath driven out of him by the crashing impact against the ground. But he had one glimpse of a squat figure, bareheaded, running up on him with pistol advanced. He could see that much, by twisting his head. But getting his Colt that far around to fire was something else.

"Where in the devil is Naile and his bunch?" he wondered, straining to cover the man, but unable to line his sights on the running figure. "They've had plenty of time . . ."

Interruption came—a flat, whip-like report. For a split second, Johnny thought that it was the running man, shooting at him. But the runner had lunged and broken stride, precisely as if someone had punched him off balance with a pole. He came on, but there was a second shot and with it his head dropped, his shoulders sagged, his knees gave. Two more paces he ran, slumping more and more, before he sprawled face downward.

"And now, me buckaroos!" Ralph Naile's cheerful bellow addressed the four at the corral. "Is there someone else that might wish to be accommodated? What? Not a devil of a fighting man amongst you? Well, then! Be dropping those hoglegs, that you pack for no reason at all, at all. Let 'em flop on the ground. We'll gather 'em all up and send 'em to the South Sea savages. *They* can use 'em for cracking coconuts and that's coconuts and coconuts beyond anything you'd ever use 'em for!"

Sid Oldfield came into the line of Johnny's vision, now. He moved to gather the dropped pistols and belts. Ralph Naile swaggered over to Johnny, looked speculatively down at the dead horse, then stooped.

"Now! And out you come when I heave him up!"

He handled the carcass as a man would flank a calf. Johnny pulled his numb leg out. He sat flexing it while High Pockets Sill and Dick Quell joined Oldfield.

"We'll take the horses," he told Ralph. "Who was it got that fellow?"

"Dick done it. We were watching, but you seemed to be doing fine and we'd not horn in. And then that drygulcher jumped you from the house and, but for much luck and Dick Quell, we'd have four to string up to the gate now!"

Johnny got up. The leg hurt, but he could limp on it. He did limp—over to the Wards. He looked grimly at them.

"I'm adding to that prophecy. Adding a warning: This country's not big enough for you two thieves and me. My advice to you is clear out! For the next time I see you, it'll be through the smoke. Who's this hairpin that committed suicide?"

"Name's Ollitt," Christy Ward said sullenly. "Don't you think you heard the last of this! We got law in this country."

"What's all this about?" a voice called from the house. "Raff? First one of your bunch that makes a funny move bites lead! I got eight men here with me and that's nine Winchesters looking at you, and all mighty light on the trigger."

Very slowly, Johnny turned toward the house, toward the sound of Nathan Hayes's familiar voice. Naile turned, too, as did Dick Quell, High Pockets Sill and Sid Oldfield. Hayes had not bluffed, for out of the little windows on this side, out of the door, as well, projected rifle or carbine barrels.

"What's it?" Ralph Naile muttered to Johnny. There was a telltale stiffening about his huge body. His blue Irish eyes were shining icily. "Do we take this, or take a chance?"

"No chance to it," Johnny mumbled sullenly. "This is the Spear, the biggest outfit in the High

Mesa country, horning in. I'm damned if I know why, but that's the Spear foreman talking. He's a big Texas roan; the real Quill, and the kind of rifleshot you read about in shorthorn story books! By himself, he could likely gather in most of us—and he's got eight salty men with him. Don't make a break! We have got to hunt a better chance."

He could not understand how the nine Spear riders had worked up to the house unseen, any more than he understood why the Spear was buying into this war. Then he raised his voice, "What are you messing into this about, Hayes?"

"I'm asking the questions, Johnny, not handing out the answers," Hayes replied calmly, "and giving out the powders, too. Number one is—grab hold of your ears, the lot of you! Pronto!"

"It's not me that'd do it!" Ralph snarled furiously.

"You damned fool!" Johnny cried shakily. "Put those paws up! Same for the rest of you!" he yelled, whirling with his own hands lifted, toward Quell, Sill and Oldfield. "This is the Spear's laugh. But—*por Dios*! I got you into this and I'll drag you out I . . ."

Nathan Hayes came lounging out of the house door. He was a handsome, swaggering figure, a shade under six feet tall, dark, lean, a savage hand-to-hand battler when it pleased him to fight barehanded, the best cowman and the best rifleshot in the High Mesa country, and, the country conceded, a gunman from who laid the chunk! Hugh Lovess trusted him and paid him accordingly.

Another cowboy followed him out of the house. Hayes grunted to this one, without taking his eyes off Johnny Raff's expression of helpless fury. His dark eyes narrowed humorously. Johnny felt that Hayes understood that it was his slip-up as a leader which infuriated him. Those Spear men should never have got up to the house. There should have been someone of Johnny's party watching. He felt that Hayes would never have slipped so.

The cowboy unbuckled the shell belt and walked on with Johnny's gun and harness. From man to man he went, taking Naile's, Quell's, Oldfield's, and Sill's weapons.

"Tough luck, Johnny," Nathan Hayes grinned. "But that's the way with lots of you boys. You aim to split the country wide open and, the more luck you have at first, the worse it turns out in the end. Puffs you up and then—*bango!* you run into a hunk of lead or rope. Happens, it'll have to be the rope in your case. Yes, sir! The old cottonwood prance. If you have got anything you want to fix up, first . . ."

Johnny stared frowningly up at him. There was something in Nathan Hayes's face, his dark eyes, that puzzled him. Why should this capture rouse the triumph he read in Hayes's expression? He had never had trouble with the foreman, during his time on the Spear. He was a top hand and Hayes was the kind of foreman who realized it. They had never exchanged anything but the most matter-of-fact words; and certainly there was nobody involved in this little war who was a friend of the big, dark, competent Texan.

Around the corner of the house rode two of the Spear men, now. They were leading the four horses of Johnny's party. Their faces were blank, hard as rocks. They pulled in. A third man rode after them. He had a bundle of lariats over his arm. Abruptly, Johnny understood.

"You lousy sneak!" he snarled at Hayes.

Without warning, then, he lifted himself to land a hard right fist with terrific force on the Spear foreman's cheekbone. He battered Hayes furiously, fighting like a wild man, never giving Hayes a chance to set himself. Back and back he pushed him. He smashed him on the fore-arm when Hayes's hand dropped beltward and knocked that hand away. He pounded him in the body. Hayes staggered. Johnny hurled himself forward to swing all the faster. Hayes sagged low enough for a fist to crash against his chin. He dropped with outflung arms. He twitched, then lay still.

Johnny jumped forward to stoop and snatch the Colts from Hayes's holsters. He got them out and began to turn. Then the world seemed to drop down upon his head. His skull exploded . . .

His head throbbed violently, when next he felt anything. But it was his neck that worried him most. He could hardly breathe. Instinctively, he tried to lift his hands to pull at whatever it was that constricted his throat. But something held his hands. Through showers of pin point sparks, daylight came back to him. He moved and swayed on whatever it was upon which he sat. Hands grasped him by the waistband of his overalls; held him steady.

He was sitting on a horse. Through the haze before his eyes, he saw turns of lariat around his arms, binding them to his body. When he moved his head, that band about his throat tightened and he opened his mouth to gasp.

But the twisting was enough to show him Ralph Naile on his horse, not a yard to the side. Ralph, too, was bound with turns of lariat, and about Ralph's neck was a noose. Johnny's eyes went upward mechanically, following the bight of the rope. It ended at the crossbar of the corral gate's frame.

"You all but had him, Johnny!" Ralph grinned. "The louse! Look at him, now! Fighting man, is it? Not a cowpenful the like of that'd trouble you, my lad! But they have got us."

"It's my fool fault!" Johnny said thickly. "I never guessed—I couldn't guess—"

"Don't you bother. It's nobody's fault. We're not blaming you."

"All ready?" Nathan Hayes's harsh voice cut in. Johnny looked at Hayes. He was not a pretty sight, with one eye swollen shut and his face covered with blood and dirt.

"Then pull those damn horses out of that! Set those sons kicking!" Hayes snarled. "Think this is a sewing circle?"

CHAPTER 10

It seemed incredible; seemed something out of a nightmare. It was not possible that he, Johnny Raff, had come to the end of the trail. But he could look into the stony face of the Spear puncher who held the horse by the bridle bit. There was nothing in that cowboy's face but grim concentration on the order Nathan Hayes had given—to pull the horses out from under the five of them who sat there under the corral gate bar.

Something very like panic rose in Johnny. He didn't want to die. Least of all did he want to die this way, with a lariat loop choking out his life, and all the plans he had made to clean up this savage, sinister gang that controlled the country's wildest section ended, too. Edward Friarson's death would never be paid for. Veck and Zagin had won.

It was no more than a second or two, that the panic had him; then red fury shook him. If he could only get to Nathan Hayes! He felt that he could walk straight into Hayes's deadly gunfire; that Hayes's lead couldn't kill him, until he had put his fingers about the Spear foreman's throat and choked him to death. He leaned a little forward against the manila that scratched his throat.

Croakingly, he cursed the tall, bloody faced

man. Cursed him with every bitter, furious oath of the cow country. The Spear foreman's battered face twisted. He jerked the Colts from his holsters and they flipped up to cover Johnny. The big hammers were back under Hayes's thumbs. Then abruptly, he let them down. He rammed the Colts back into the holsters.

"You can't beat the rope that way," he said between his teeth. His hands jerked. He roared at the cowboys who sat on their horses at the heads of the animals which held up Johnny, Quell, Ralph Naile, Sid Oldfield and High Pockets Sill.

There was a terrific jerk at his neck, then Johnny found himself strangling in air. The weight of his body tightened the noose. The rope was cutting into his stiffened neck, stopping his breath. Already, it was agony to suck in and expel air. He fought to get his hands loose and with his struggles the noose tightened. His head was swelling; there was a dull roaring like a waterfall in his ears. Sparks flew before his protruding eyes; showers of them; spangling the blackness that had swallowed up the light of day. He had the illusion of falling, of dropping to earth with a heavy thud. Then blankness came.

High pitched voices, furious voices, from far away came slowly closer. A man's voice, deep, angry, and a thinner voice. It could have been a woman's. Except, in this blackness that still surrounded him, where would a woman be? The iron band still pressed in his windpipe. Johnny Raff knew that this was all illusion; he was hanging to the cross bar of the corral gate; he was choking to death. He flung up his hands—and this time they were not held to his sides. He touched his throat. There was no rope there. He opened his eyes, but light dazzled him so that he could not see. He shut them again and sprawled on the ground, fingering his neck.

"I'm foreman of the Spear!" the man's voice came clearly to him. "What I say goes, Elenore. Your pa has told you, before . . ."

"Hugh Lovess is not playing the Ring's game. He's not hanging Martinez's enemies for him. And, remember that after all you're *nothing* but a hired hand of the Spear, Nathan Hayes, the same as these cowboys! And don't forget the other little message—any of you! The first man who makes a move toward Johnny Raff or these others—by God! I'll kill him like a mad coyote!"

This time, when he opened his eyes, Johnny could see. He lay just outside of the corral gate. He saw Elenore Lovess's booted legs beyond him. And the *chivarrias* of her *vaquero* escort. There was rigidity about all those legs, placed a yard apart in a kind of line. Johnny lifted his eyes.

The Spear cowboys and the Wards and the two 77 punchers were grouped before Elenore and the grim faced, rifle armed Mexicans. A hand fell on Johnny's shoulder. A voice croaked in his ear:

"Johnny, me lad!" Ralph Naile said raspingly. "You're out of it? I gather that the young lady fogged up in bare time to be cutting the ropes and letting us drop. And your friend, the foreman, he's not pleased at all, at all."

Johnny turned painfully, to find that Quell, Oldfield and Sill were sitting up. Their hands were at their necks, where red circles told of the rope's work.

"Johnny," Elenore said tightly over her shoulder, "there's a bottle in my saddlebags. I think you all need a drink."

Johnny got shakily to his feet. The corral spun and whirled before him for a dizzy instant, then straightened. He walked over to Elenore's black and groped in the *alforjas* until he found the quart. He handed it to Ralph Naile, who jerked the cork and took a big drink. Oldfield, Quell, and High Pockets stumbled over. They drank. Johnny killed the rest.

Johnny felt almost normal, except for the pain in his throat. He straightened, looked around, found a carbine in scuffed scabbard, hanging to the corral bars. The property of one of the 77 punchers, he thought. He slid inside the corral and pulled it from the scabbard. It was loaded. He walked back outside and stood beside Elenore.

"You lost this one," he told Nathan Hayes, hoarsely. "I don't know what made you buy into this fight that's none of the Spear's war. But I'll probably find it out, in time. Now, we're going to leave you."

He spoke over his shoulder to Ralph Naile, still watching Hayes.

"Ralph, I see our hardware, stacked over yonder. You go get it. Hayes, I hope nobody makes a funny move while the boys are recovering their property, because somebody'll certainly get killed. You can maybe figure it out for yourself, that I've got no particular reason to be light on the trigger when my Winchester's pointing toward you!"

Hayes's battered face was a mask of impotent fury. But, as Johnny had said, he had lost this throw. He could hardly expect Hugh Lovess to back him up, if he opened fire on Elenore and the two *vaqueros*, whose sole, ordered duty in life was to do without question whatever Elenore commanded. And, if a gun battle were staged now, flying lead might hit her. No . . . this was not Nathan Hayes's day, and the Spear foreman was not used to being beaten. His hands clenched and unclenched. Johnny nodded grimly. "Don't like it, huh? Well, I'll tell you something more: There's going to be a lot happening around this High Mesa country that you won't like a little bit. I'm not a forgiving soul, 'specially. And if I was, that still wouldn't help you! Get your horses, boys!"

He found himself, five minutes later, sitting a horse which Ralph Naile had ridden calmly into the corral to rope out of those O-Dots. Nor had anyone said a word of objection—not the Wards, nor either of the 77 men. Johnny rode over to Elenore Lovess. She seemed oddly ill at ease. It was in no way like the usual manner of the Crown Princess of the great Spear outfit. She found difficulty in meeting his eyes.

"Elenore . . ." said Johnny slowly. "Elenore . . . talk's no good, in a thing like this. If it hadn't been for you . . ."

"Don't talk about it! It—it was too horrible!" she stopped him. "I couldn't have done anything else." She seemed to get control of herself, then. She lifted those level, dark blue eyes, which had played such havoc with Johnny Raff's peace of mind while he worked on the Spear. She looked straight into his face. "I couldn't have done less for one of Nacho Howze's Mexican sheep herders, Johnny. You ought to see that, for it was the Spear that did that. Dad's hard handed, but he wouldn't tolerate this sort of business for a minute. As for Nathan Hayes saying you'd rustled Spear stuff—that's simply silly. Now, I want you to come away with us."

In a tight little bunch, Johnny and Ralph, Quell and Oldfield and High Pockets Sill rode away from the quiet corral, behind the grimly silent bunch of Spear men, at whose head rode Nathan

Hayes, and behind which Elenore and her two *vaqueros* trailed.

They were six or seven miles along the trail to the Spear when suddenly Elenore whirled her horse with a grunt to the Mexicans. They looked at her and continued on their course. She rode back to Johnny and stopped her horse.

"Fall back and side me, Johnny," she said evenly. "I have to talk to you."

He reined back to let the others pass him. Then, fifty yards in their rear, he and Elenore rode stirrup to stirrup.

"Johnny," the girl said earnestly, "you're riding to a fall. I can see it, if you can't. Granted that everything you believe is true. Granted that the Ring's crooked as a snake's trail and that it runs the High Mesa country clear up to the capital—with the help of a shorthorn child of a governor.

"You can't lick the Ring. They have all the county officers in their hip pockets. Whatever they do is legal and right. Whatever you do is illegal, criminal. Don't you see that? Don't you know that every peace officer in the county, and the United States marshals, all of them, will be after you; that you're going to be caught and tried and sentenced to be hung, not to a corral gate, but legally! You're an outlaw! Now, if you're even a little bit grateful to me, for what I did back there, do something for me. Get out of the High Mesa country, Johnny. Go back to Texas. Go anywhere, while you have a chance. You've accomplished something. You've made those rascals shiver, at Mesita—maybe clear up to Aden."

"That is not enough!" Johnny said grimly. "Not near enough! Before the bullet that's named for me, or the rope, comes up to wherever I happen to be, there's going to be shivering done that will make it look like Veck and Zagin and Greathouse were standing stock still the other day, when you thought they were shivering."

He hunched his shoulders and stared blindly at the riders ahead of them. If Elenore looked at him, he paid no heed to it. He was putting his jumbled thoughts into order.

CHAPTER 11

"Johnny! Johnny!" she said impatiently, after a half mile of silence. "Are you deaf?"

"What? No, I was thinking, about this business—all the whole mess. I told you the other day on the trail, just before we ran into that shooting posse, how I felt toward Edward Friarson. Now, I feel like I've inherited this war; Friarson's war. I'm a lot better fixed to carry it on than he ever was. I'm going to try to do what Ed wanted done.

"Yes, sir! I aim to clean up this den of sidewinders. I owe you whatever my neck's worth, Elenore. It makes me feel like doing whatever you ask me to do. But shucks! You know what sent me off the Spear. You knew well enough how I felt toward you, then. You could've asked me to do anything, and I'd have run to charge hell with a bucket of water. But—this is different. If I am wiped out, I'm wiped out. That's that. But I never will forget what I'm owing you, Elenore."

She stared incredulously at him. He leaned across to put his hands upon hers, where it rested on the saddlehorn. She pulled, but he held her.

"So I can't hightail. No matter what you say, you'd know I was wrong to run. I'm not running. I'm sticking and I'm fighting. Maybe I'm dying, too. I can't tell. But after the smoke's blown away, if 'm able, and it looks right, I will be around to see you, to ask you something."

"Don't trouble yourself!" she cried angrily. "I answered you, once, on the Spear, when you forgot yourself."

Johnny jerked his hand away as from a hot coal. She rammed the hooks to her horse and was gone at furious gallop. She passed Ralph Naile and the others with a swirl of sand from her horse's hoofs. They turned to gape at her; turned still around to gape at Johnny. He beckoned them.

"Let 'em go!" he said between his teeth. "To hell with the Spear! We'll cut across the hog-back yonder. When we're out of sight of Nathan Hayes, we'll head straight back for the 77. I reckon Christy and Oliver Ward think we're discouraged. Hell! What *they* don't know!"

The Spear party vanished. Johnny rode by a long loop, until with darkness almost upon them, they drew up once more on a hillcrest, over which lay the desolate, square adobe of Walt Jefferies of the 77.

"I have changed my mind, some," Johnny said meditatively to the others. "I aimed to ride into that corral and run out our O-Dots. But now . . . come on, you mesquite hoppers!"

They made the motte of cottonwoods as Ralph Naile and the others had made it, earlier in the day. They could hear voices out at the horse corral. Evidently the Wards and those two 77 riders believed that Johnny Raff's going had been permanent; that they had nothing more to worry about.

The four of them were in and around the corral when Johnny led his bunch in at a quiet walk, around the corner of the house. Johnny grunted to Sid Oldfield, "Let's don't make any more bobbles, Sid. Slide inside and round up the place, then, keep your eye skinned for the back. Don't let anybody take us from behind, again."

The Wards whirled at the gate, when Johnny stopped his horse to look meditatively across at them. Christy's dropping chin was quite apparent, across forty yards of space. But Oliver—Johnny watched Oliver closely. He had not changed his opinion of the two. Oliver would be the stayer, the fighter.

And Oliver, now, bore out that opinion, for he dropped his hand to his six-shooter and jumped for the gate. At Johnny's elbow, a Winchester *whanged!* Oliver dropped and lay motionless. Johnny yelled at Christy and spurred forward. He yelled, also, at the two 77 men inside with the horses; yelled that they would not be hurt if they didn't fight. They came slowly outside, hands ostentatiously at shoulder level.

"See what's the bill on Oliver," Johnny grunted to one of them. Then he looked at Christy and said, "Well, now . . . about the horses . . ."

"Gone!" the 77 man grunted tersely, rising from Oliver's shoulder.

"That was murder!" Christy panted. "Plumb murder! You damn nigh hung this morning. But you won't miss it, next time!"

He showed no concern about Oliver's death; his greenish eyes never went to Oliver's body. He was scared stiff, but at the same time, he seemed to expect that a bluff would work on Johnny Raff.

"I aimed to take the Friarson horses," Johnny drawled, crooking a leg around his saddlehorn, the better to make a cigarette. "But now—hell, I'd just have to sell 'em, anyhow. And why go hunting a buyer when here you are, right on the ground. Now! Now!" he interrupted Christy's fierce oath of protest. "Don't use up your language where it won't do you any good. You're elected. Yes, sir! Voice of the people—I'm the people, Christy. Leastways, I'm the people you'd better worry about."

"Them's my horses!" Christy cried shrilly. "Don't you think you can come running a sandy over me!"

"Hell, I wouldn't run a sandy over you," Johnny said dreamily, staring down at the long-nosed face. "I wouldn't even bluff you, Christy. No! When I tell you that either I'll sell you the O-Dots in the corral or string you up to that crossbar you know so much about, I'm not bluffing! Simon Jones, he thought I was bluffing him, yesterday in the Congress at Mesita, and he knows better, now. So does Tigre Lopez!"

"You—You mean to try to tell me you downed Lopez and Jones? I don't believe no such thing!"

"Your hard luck! Now, I don't know what shrinkage there has been, but there was around fifty head of good horses on the O-Dot when Kesall and Company raided the place. I figure forty dollars'd square things. Forty a head, you know. Say, two thousand, just to keep it even, and I know you're packing that much in gold. So, Christy, this is one time you'll make an honest trade . . ."

Christy began a furious tirade. He would do no such thing. He had already paid for those horses.

"Tchk!" said Johnny, gently. "Knowing they were stolen, too. And you admit it before witnesses!"

A loop came out like a darting snake's head, from where Ralph Naile sat in the group behind Johnny. It caught Christy Ward about his long neck. Ralph's well-trained horse kept the lariat taut, no matter how Christy danced and fought to snatch it off.

"I'll pay it!" he gasped at last. "It's robbery! You'll swing for killing Oliver, the whole bunch of you! And you'll be charged with highway robbery."

"They can't be hanging us twice, though,"

Ralph Naile objected. "How will you straighten that?"

He led Christy to his saddle and kept the lariat stiff while the trader fished in a saddlebag and, with many groans, counted out two thousand dollars in gold. Johnny rode up to the pair and grinned at Christy Ward.

"You still feel like you've been robbed? Aim to run to Greathouse and tell him I held you up for two thousand?"

"You know damn well I do!" Christy snarled. His green eyes were like the eyes of a trodden snake.

"Well, then . . . I know where you aim to sell the O-Dots . . . news does travel. I'll tell you what you already ought to know: Platt won't buy that bunch of horses from you—not without an O-Dot bill of sale. You won't hoorah *him* into believing they're recovered this and that, with an O-Dot blotted onto something or other. No, sir! Platt wouldn't touch a horse he wasn't sure about, and there's no other place you can sell 'em, quick!"

"What are you driving at?" Christy's eyes narrowed, now. He watched Johnny just as malignantly, but there was puzzlement in his long-nosed face, his green eyes, now. "Not that I'm telling you what I aimed to do with the horses."

"If this is a robbery, then what's to hinder me taking the horses and selling 'em to Platt? I'm still foreman of the O-Dot. Until somebody takes charge of the estate, I have got the right to sell off O-Dot stock and give bills of sale. I can give Platt one. He knows me. And if I'm robbing you, I might as well *rob* you! But if you want to sit down and write out that you bought fifty head of O-Dot horses from me—the foreman that represents the Friarson estate, at forty a head . . ."

Christy Ward saw the trap. He glared at Johnny in balked fury, while Ralph Naile beat his thigh gently and rocked in the saddle, with mouth wide open and eyes closed, laughing soundlessly.

"You got me!" Christy snarled. "It's a hold-up, all the same, but I got to knuckle under. But this ain't the end of the business, don't you ever think it is!"

He fished a greasy notebook from the pocket of his coat and used the seat of his saddle for steady rest and with the stub of a pencil scrawled upon a page torn from the book. He handed it over with an angry jerk. Johnny read it carefully and nodded and placed it carefully in his pocket. Then he held out his hand for the notebook and pencil.

He wrote, in the round copy book letters Edward Friarson had taught him to make, but he did not hand over the bill of sale. He looked down at Christy Ward and hummed absently. Then he lifted his voice to yell, "Dick Quell! Bring the two 77 boys over here!"

When they stood staring sulkily from him to

Ward, he addressed them softly, "Christy has been thinking things over. He has decided to buy the O-Dots in the corral, taking my bill of sale to cover the deal, and giving me a certificate that I can turn over to the Friarson estate. Thinking never comes easy to Christy, but I tell you, when he starts, he's liable to end up just anywhere! He went right along thinking, Christy did, and when he got done thinking how much better it'd be to have a bill of sale on the Friarson horses, he never stopped. No, sir! He got to thinking how Oliver started for his gun and was going to smoke us up, and he's afraid somebody, later on, might get a wrong idea about the deal. So he wants you-all to witness the paper he's going to write, saying that Oliver had his hand on a gun and aimed to shoot us poor innocent O-Dot men, when he was killed."

"Like hell I do!" Christy yelled again. "But I'll sign it! I'll write it down for a good deed—damn your soul! I ain't going to lose two thousand because that idiot tried to open a war, when he wasn't sure he could get you!"

"Tell these boys how it is," Johnny suggested. "You want to write it all down because of the kindness you feel for me and the rest of the O-Dots. You don't want a mistake made by Greathouse or anybody . . ."

"Sure! Oliver had it coming to him," Christy snarled viciously. "He was going to down Raff and these others, and they beat him to it! Sure! I'll put it all down."

Presently, when one 77 puncher had painfully signed the paper as a witness, and the other had made his mark, Johnny nodded. "And that's that—thanks to meeting Walt Jefferies in Mesita. I don't like a lot of the company Walt travels with, and lets come into his corrals, but he never holds with downright stealing. So there's hope for him yet."

"Walt Jefferies!" Ward cried and made the name sound like an oath. "Did Walt Jefferies tell you them O-Dot horses were here?"

"Oh, no! No! He never said a word about 'em!" Johnny cried quickly and artistically. "I ran into him at Mesita. That was all. We—we got to talking some. We—why, maybe he didn't know even that Kesall had pushed 'em over here, at all!"

CHAPTER 12

Ralph Naile beat his thigh ecstatically, as the five of them rode away from the 77.

"Oh, man!" he gasped. "But his face, when you were springing the clearance paper on him . . . You should be Irish for the kind of head you've got on you."

"Likely that paper wouldn't be worth a whoop in court," Johnny grinned, "but maybe Christy'll figure he's well off, with Oliver's share of the business in his pocket. They do say that there's four men in the country Christy couldn't skin: Zeke Martinez up at Aden, Veck and Zagin, and Oliver Ward. He won't be on such terms with the 77—not after my little slip of the tongue about meeting Walt Jefferies—to ask Walt Jeffries to send the two punchers into court to testify against us."

"I would say you had about signed a death warrant for Jefferies," Dick Quell nodded grimly.

"I wouldn't say that," Johnny disagreed, dreamily. "I would rather say that there'll maybe be a little bitsy hard feeling, and that Walt Jefferies'll find himself lined up against the Ring, and wondering how the hell he came to be there."

He led them through the darkness that came shortly, by trails well known to him, skirting the foothills. The moon was up when he stopped before an old stone house at Rojo Canon, Red Canon, on the range of Nacho Howze, the half breed sheep king.

"I reckon we're safe to stretch our weary bones, now," he told them. "Nobody uses this place much. Used to be an outlaw hangout. One night the gang had a woman they'd captured in a raid; I don't know much about her. They were about six strong, and they started playing cards for her. All anybody knows is that one of Nacho's herders found her running barefoot across the range, next morning. When they came to look into this house, they found the whole bunch dead—shot and hacked to pieces. You couldn't pile up money enough to hire a Mex' to be inside a mile of this house, after dark."

"What became of the woman?" Ralph Naile inquired, somewhat later, when they had a cooking fire blazing inside the old house and the horses stamped in a roofless room adjoining. Dick Quell and High Pockets were cooking supper. "Crazy. Her folks came after her. The Mex' say you can hear the gang riding up to the house, here, sometimes on a quiet night, and whenever you hear it, somebody's going to die. They're great for starting tales like that. Point is, nobody much ever comes around here. We're not apt to be seen."

They ate and sprawled on the saddle blankets

smoking. Ralph Naile yarned of wild days along the Border; of a range war in which he and Sid Oldfield and High Pockets Sill had fought. Johnny put in a word here and there, but he was not really thinking of what Ralph said. His mind was running from point to point of his problems, and to the lovely, self-willed face of Elenore Lovess. "You'd think I was a greaser," he told himself. "Way she acts. Well, I'll pay her back, somehow. Then she can . . ."

"*Madre de Dios*!" Ralph Naile gasped, stopping short in what he was saying. "Horses coming!"

Johnny jerked upright and listened, and heard a clear, unmistakable thudding, the pound of hoofs. One horse or more, he could not say. He looked sidelong at the others. It was Sid Oldfield's face that caught his eyes. Oldfield's face was strained and ghastly, in the flicker of the fire's light; his single blue eye seemed to bulge from the socket.

"I—I don't give a damn . . ." Oldfield seemed to be thinking aloud, rather than addressing anyone, ". . . for what I can *see,* what's human . . ."

"Hell!" Johnny laughed, if strainedly. "You don't think that's our gang of ghosts riding? Likely it's somebody anxious to leave this neighborhood in a hurry."

The hoofs suddenly seemed to bear off to the left—to Johnny's left. They died away. Sid Oldfield wiped his face with shirt sleeves. He snarled when Ralph Naile laughed amusedly, "Go on!

Laugh! You Mick hyena! Something walked across my grave, then, I tell you. What's solid and I can see, I ain't worried a bit about, and you know it damn well from the Border. But *that* kind of spooky business . . ."

Ralph took up his story again, and Johnny returned to his meditations. Dick Quell and Sill were silent; neither was much of a talker. An hour passed. Sill's head was bobbling; Dick Quell was snoring. From outside there was a sound of a scuffing foot. Johnny's hand slid to the butt of his Colt. It came out as he wiggled into the shadows by the wall and moved soundlessly toward the gaping doorway, through which the moon shone.

"Raff! Johnny Raff!" a nervous voice called.

"Who's it?" Johnny replied suspiciously.

"Mollison. All right to come inside?"

He came in, with Johnny's grunt of assent. All stared curiously at his gangling, shabby figure, his small, beard-stubbled face.

"Johnny," he said slowly, licking a corn husk cigarette, "did Friarson sell Veck and Zagin my paper—my mortgage, I mean? I couldn't think he did, but Jink Kesall came to me yesterday and says he's expecting to be sent to foreclose on me, unless I scrape up a thousand."

"Why a thousand?" Johnny demanded and scowled. "The mortgage on the Flying M was for twenty-one hundred. Anyhow, Edward Friarson never sold Veck and Zagin a thing. *I* know where they got hold of that mortgage, though: Kesall broke into Friarson's box at the O-Dot. Likely, he took all of Friarson's papers. Did Kesall offer you the mortgage for a thousand?"

"Yeah! He says Friarson sold at less than half to Veck and Zagin, and they want to cash the paper. Friarson told me, just last week, that it was going to be all right to renew!"

"Well, don't you pay 'em a cent! If you do, you're going to pay twice. The Friarson estate owns all the mortgages that Friarson wrote, and their stealing 'em won't clear up a thing. You sit tight. If Kesall comes out, tell him you can't raise the money."

"But if he comes out with a killing posse, Johnny, to foreclose? What'll I do? *I* can't fight the county!"

Johnny looked thoughtfully at him. Mollison was much like Lewis Talbot, he reflected; like the storekeeper partner of Edward Friarson, Mollison had a family to consider. He was a poor man and had no name as a fighter. Johnny wondered if Mollison could be depended upon—in what degree he would stand hitched. But, if the skittish honest ranchers would line up, opposed to Veck, Zagin, Greathouse and the rest of the Ring . . .

"Looks like I'm rammed right into rodding the fight to down that bunch," he told Mollison. "All right! I'll take on the job! And if you'll side us—make whatever play you're called on to make, to slam the Martinez Monkeys, I'll promise you this much: You won't be foreclosed on, and you won't have to try killing off any posse coming to foreclose. Is that fair enough for you?"

Mollison stared doubtfully at Johnny. The corn husk cigarette, jerking in his mouth, told of his indecision. "But, Johnny—it's mightily easy to say that. But how do I know you can deliver? I got a family. I'd be a damn sight better off, if you think about it, to put the old lady and the kids into the wagon and move out and let 'em take the Flying M and start over again. It's better'n getting killed and leaving 'em to be throwed off!"

"Yeah. If it was like that. But all I can tell you is this: I've already twisted Veck and Zagin's partnership tail. Maybe you have heard about the Martinez Monkeys—Monty Greathouse rats—marching into the Congress, and about Simon Jones and Tigre Lopez, and today's little business at the 77? All right! I have made Veck and Zagin pay me six hundred for the damage done at the O-Dot, and today I made Christy Ward pay me two thousand for the fifty head of O-Dots that Kesall ran off the ranch and sold the Wards."

"I didn't know about the money, either place!" Mollison said amazedly. "It just don't hardly seem possible!"

"They felt like that, too," Johnny nodded, very dryly, "but I have got twenty-six hundred, right here. Now, some few have tried to buck the

Martinez Ring, but they never really got started. I'm bucking it and I ask you—who's ahead? Johnny Raff, or Greathouse and Veck and Zagin? You reckon I can protect you?"

"Looks kind of like it! Yet . . . looks mightily like it, and if you could beat 'em, it'd be the saving of the country."

CHAPTER 13

Sid Oldfield stirred, where he had sprawled motionless on his blanket. His one blue eye was very bright as he regarded the Flying M owner. "Was that you galloping towards the house an hour or more back?" he asked strainedly.

"No," said Mollison, staring. "I was going mighty quiet, aiming to look for Johnny on the O-Dot. Then I seen a fire shining—I must've seen it a half mile off, when I topped out of an arroyo. It came to me that Johnny might be here. No, I wasn't galloping."

He stood up. There was still uncertainty in the set of his narrow shoulders, but by no means so much as had been there at first. He looked Johnny steadily in the eye as he put out a long, gnarled hand. "I have got the family to think about, Johnny," he said apologetically. "If I was a single man, I'd be riding with you and sticking to the last cartridge. But I'll promise you this much: Anything I *can* do to smack the—what do you call 'em, Martinez Monkeys—that I'll do! If it just don't look like it's hopeless; like I'd get killed to no good end."

When he had gone, they lay for a while before the dying fire. Johnny nodded slightly at last. "I'm going to take those mortgages away from

Veck and Zagin," he told Ralph Naile, the only one still awake. "Yes sir! I am that! You know, Ralph, it's not right, their taking papers and things that don't belong to 'em out of Friarson's strongbox; It's—why, it's plumb wicked."

"You don't say!" Ralph cried, amazed. "Then by all means, let's be getting 'em back. I cannot stand a wicked man, you little devil! We'll be smacking 'em."

They were awake well before dawn. The morning was chill, at that altitude. Sid Oldfield picked up a water bag, yawning. There was a spring trickling from the arroyo wall, fifty yards from the stone house. Oldfield went outside without stopping to buckle on his shell belt or tie about his thigh the toe string of the holster that carried his long, wooden handled Colt. He went out with shoulders hunched in the dingy black coat he wore, with one pant leg in, one out, of his boot-legs.

Johnny built up the fire from embers in the ashes. Ralph Naile yawned and reached for a chunk of bacon. Dick Quell had the tin can that served as a coffee pot. High Pockets Sill sat cross-legged on his blanket, rolling a cigarette. Then a rattle of shots sounded from somewhere about the spring.

Johnny dropped a mesquite root and jumped to the door. From it he could look straight along the arroyo toward the spring. Over the arroyo's rim, there were rifle barrels projecting. Little wisps of smoke still curled upward. Sid Oldfield, still clinging to the goatskin water bag, came at a staggering run toward the cabin's door. The rifles rattled hollowly again. The echoes rebounded from the far wall of the arroyo. Sid Oldfield fell flat upon his face but came scrambling up again. Johnny snatched his carbine from where it leaned against the wall by the door.

He sent a half-dozen shots toward the rifle barrels, and they disappeared with jerky abruptness. Sid Oldfield's black coat flapped back. The front of his gray shirt was crimson now. His mouth was open. But his blue eye shone like ice from his contorted face.

"Gimme my cutter!" he was gasping. "I'm done for! But I'll get one of the illegitimates—before I cash!"

"Come inside, you idiot!" Ralph Naile bellowed.

But Oldfield stood stubbornly, outside, with hand outstretched for his Colt. Ralph jumped to where it lay on Oldfield's blanket. He jumped back to the door with it. Oldfield took it, then turned and went at a staggering trot toward a narrow path that led from the arroyo bottom.

From behind the stone house came more shots. Sill went to the tiny window there and opened up on the men. Dick Quell joined him. Johnny and Ralph, covering the front, were fascinated by the sight of Oldfield, clinging desperately to rock and bush on that little goat path. They saw him top out of the arroyo at last, to drop flat. They heard the roar of his pistol, followed quickly by a volley from the hidden riflemen. A man jumped to his feet, where those rifle barrels had been. His head was back. His hand clawed at his throat. He fell over the arroyo rim and rolled to the bottom, and Sid Oldfield's limp body came sliding, feet first, into the rut of the path, to bounce outward and drop to the sand and gravel of the arroyo floor. It lay motionless, fingers still gripping the wooden stock of the Colt.

"He was a salty hairpin!" Ralph grunted. "He got one to pay for the killing of him!"

The fire jumped now from four points—front, back, and both sides. With a rock, Ralph smashed out a porthole in the blank side wall. Dick Quell slid into the ruined room that sheltered the horses. He opened up from behind the remnant of the wall there.

Presently, the besiegers' fire slackened. Johnny heard someone yelling from the arroyo rim. He listened until he identified the voice as Greathouse's.

"What do you want?" he yelled in reply.

"You come on out of that, now! Drop your guns and come out. I've got twenty men."

"What do you mean—twenty men!" Johnny interrupted him. "Likely, you have got about ten men and the rest skunks like you and Eddieford and Jink Kesall! You don't think we'd surrender to the likes of you, Greathouse! You'd better take your drygulching murderers and hightail. Else some more of you will be hurt. I'm warning you!"

A volley rattled without warning, sending lead to sing and whine as it glanced off the rock walls around the door. But Johnny had not been so foolish as to show himself.

Presently, the sun came out, and with the intermittent firing, the morning wore on. Dick Quell reported that High Pockets's horse was dead, killed by a glancing bullet. Ralph Naile went into the stable room and, with Quell helping, threw and hobbled the rest of the horses to get them down out of the line of fire.

Noon came. The firing ceased. Ralph pushed the cold beans forward. "My mouth's like a lime kiln!" he grinned mockingly. "Poor old Sid! He died thirsty, too. Looks much as if we would die of thirst before that careful bunch will come close enough to kill us!"

A determined attack was made, simultaneously, on the four sides, early in the afternoon. But Dick Quell killed one of the posse on his side, and on front and back and Ralph Naile's side, the others sent so hot a return fire that the sheriff's men dropped down behind boulders and lay flat, with lead all but burning their ears. Those who had not gotten down into the arroyo pulled back away from the rim.

Johnny squinted through the door at the sun. He nodded to himself and spoke to Ralph without turning, “Come dark, I’m going to slide out, straight down the arroyo past the spring. I’ll whang away at ’em from that side, and the rest of you’ll come out, riding the same way. Sill, you take my horse. I’ll gather up one from some posseman. I think Greathouse is aiming to starve us out.”

“Your damn gizzard’ll be looking like a sieve before you ever got started!” Ralph cried scornfully. “You have to pass that bunch lying behind the rocks.”

“Ah, you’re just crazy! Me, I’m a full-blood Comanche Indian, half-Apache and half-Liver Regulator. I’m a Texas Man, you big Mick. ’Leven foot tall and I heft nine hundred. If any of that bunch rises up in my path, I’ll just *blow* at him, and he’ll frizzle. You’ll bring the horses in here, come dark, and saddle up. When I open up the ball from the side they won’t be expecting trouble from, you come out hell for leather!”

They argued with him bitterly. But all were very thirsty. Another twelve or fifteen hours without water would bc torture, and it seemed that Greathouse depended upon their surrendering because of lack of water, preferring the slower, safer method of siege to another attack.

There was very little shooting before darkness came. Johnny saw Ralph Naile and Sill and Quell unhobble the three living horses and lead them into the room. Then he slid out of the door. His carbine was tied to his back with a saddle string. His Colt was in his hand. He made the shelter of a boulder, twelve or fifteen feet from the doorway, then stopped to listen. From somewhere near the spring, he heard the mutter of voices. He crawled silently on. A man grunted, a startled sound, from his left.

"They're mighty quiet," Johnny muttered and the man made a grunting noise of assent. "Where's Monty?" Johnny asked.

"Spring, I reckon. Like they wish they was!"

Johnny laughed quite naturally, for he felt like laughing. He wriggled on through the darkness, from boulder to boulder. Two more men he passed. To both, he grunted what he had told the first man, that the men in the stone house were very quiet. One he knew as a D-Bar man, Phil Carr. Then, at last, he heard the gurgle of the spring, where its tiny stream splashed over the smooth, worn boulder that made its basin. There were dark figures standing there, clear against gray rocks.

"Who's it?" Monty Greathouse challenged him suspiciously when Johnny stood and slouched toward the water.

"Phil Carr," Johnny mumbled, coming on. He

dropped at Greathouse's very feet, to bury his face in the water. He drank noisily.

"They'll hear you clean up to the house!" Jink Kesall told him sourly. Then, absently, "Wonder how many's left in the house?"

"Now, don't you fret, Jink," Greathouse said quickly. "They will be damn dry, come morning. By noon—hell! They'll be coming out begging us to let 'em surrender. No sense to making a fool rush and being killed."

"Lot of risk you'd run!" Kesall snarled. "You wouldn't be up in the front line, Monty. You damn well know it!"

Johnny lifted himself. He felt much better now. He stood and went slouching past the three of them. Greathouse called after him, asking where he was going. Johnny mumbled the one word "saddle" and kept on walking.

"Oh, Carr!" Greathouse called again. "Carr! Wait a minute!"

"What do you want?" the real Carr demanded from where he was lying behind his boulder.

Johnny leaped forward. Behind him, at the spring, rose a confused babble, but one came running after him. He turned to slam a couple of shots at this one—Kesall, he guessed, then he scrambled up the arroyo bank. On its rim, with bullets picking the hard ground around him, he jerked his Winchester from the tie string. He raked the arroyo with lead.

Then up he came and ran off to the left, where he guessed the posse's horses would be. Men jumped up and he told them in an excited voice that the gang in the house was trying to break out. He was going for more cartridges.

CHAPTER 14

He fairly cannoned into the horses, standing unsaddled in the hollow. Nobody was with them now; all the posse had run toward the arroyo rim. Johnny selected a saddle by sense of touch. He measured the stirrup leathers with his arm, found them near enough the proper length, then picked a horse by the same method. He swung up into the saddle.

From down the arroyo came wild yells. Ralph Naile's Irish howl would have carried a half-mile against the wind. Sill and Dick Quell swelled the noise. There was a blaze of shooting, then the thud of hoofs. Johnny swung down again, slashing the ropes that held the grazing posse horses. With a yell, he started them off and choused them forward, then rode back toward the arroyo, toward the spot where the yelling now sounded loudest. He opened up wildly with the carbine, firing at random toward the arroyo rim.

He yelled for Ralph and got no answer. Two minutes later, he pulled in the borrowed horse among the others. He turned in the saddle to face the posse, which fired as wildly, now, as he had blazed away a moment before.

"Oh, Greathouse!" he yelled again and again, until the shooting died away. "Greathouse! Come out from under that rock! If you want us, come see us on the Bronco! But bring plenty! We'll be waiting for you, all uncoupled!"

"And where is this Bronco?" Ralph inquired as they jogged off.

"Northeast. But don't let geography get you down, my son, for we're heading for Mesita now. You see, Ralph, me, I'm a full-blooded Comanche Indian . . ."

"Sure! I know that one. All Comanche, but the part of you that's Damned Fool is far and away the biggest part. But where do we drink?"

They watered the thirsty horses and themselves drank, in a little creek that Johnny told them was named by the Mexicans "The Stream of the Lost Spirit."

"Don't be talking about spirits!" Ralph cried. "Poor Sid Oldfield believed in 'em, you recall, he had a foreseeing, last night. Something walking across his grave, he says, and, by the powers, something walking over his grave it was!"

They went at alternating lope and foxtrot, toward Mesita. It was nearly dawn when they came to the county seat's edge. Johnny left the three in a brush-crowned arroyo while he rode boldly toward the rear of Judge Kent Biddle's house. He passed the corrals and stables and swung down at the back door of the house. He knew the Judge's bedroom, so he walked into the darkened patio and tapped on the door.

"Johnny Raff!" he answered Biddle's challenge. "I have got a little stuff in my saddlebags that belongs to the Friarson estate."

Biddle unbarred the door, and Johnny went in. Biddle lit a lamp and stood in nightshirt and slippers, staring at the stubbled, dirty, haggard cowboy.

"Johnny . . . I don't know what to say to you!" he confessed helplessly. "I don't know whether you're going to start a war that will get us all killed, and leave the Martinez Ring in control, or . . ."

Johnny grinned mirthlessly. Very briefly, he told of holding Veck and Zagin up for six hundred; of the affair at the 77; and of the sale of the O-Dot horses to Christy Ward.

"So Oliver's dead," Biddle nodded. "Good riddance! A lot of people would have killed Christy, but for fear of Oliver. Now . . . so you have twenty-six hundred to turn over to the estate?"

"Yeah, but I'm going to turn over just sixteen hundred, right now. I need a thousand for a little while. It's . . . well, I have got a notion . . ."

"I know your notions well enough, by now, not to ask or argue," Biddle nodded, "but isn't Greathouse and his gang apt to pop into town?"

"I didn't think to tell you," Johnny grinned. "I ran off their horses. They will have quite a walk. Has Talbot been bothered any?"

"Plenty! And that reminds me: Did Friarson

have his mortgages at the ranch? He did! I thought he must have had them there and that Kesall and his gang took them. Because Veck and Zagin sent word to Talbot that they hold his paper for five thousand. They claim to have bought it, quite secretly, from Friarson. They're going to foreclose on the store. It isn't legal, of course, but with all the county officials working for them . . ."

He snapped his fingers hopelessly. Johnny nodded quietly.

"It's about those mortgages, that I have got my notion."

He went out, with Biddle following him. He gave Biddle the buckskin sack holding sixteen hundred. He dumped a thousand dollars in gold into a saddlebag. Then he grinned down at Biddle from the saddle.

"See you later, Judge," he said. "Anyhow, I hope so!"

He rode around the corner of the house and out upon the road. He turned boldly down it, toward the square house of Zagin, where the fat "moccasin" lived with his Mexican wife and brood of half-breed children. Again, he knew the lay of the land, for he had come here many times for orders when he rode for Veck and Zagin. He rode into the patio and swung off at Zagin's bedroom door. He rapped on the heavy wood.

"Kesall!" he said harshly, when Zagin spoke

sleepily from just the other side of the barrier. "Hell's to pay!"

Presently, the door opened. Zagin came out mumbling:

"Always hell to pop, with Monty Greathouse. Always . . . Ah! Johnny! You pays us the visit, no? Fi-ine, Johnny!"

But hollow blue eyes were roving, roving, to cover the empty, quiet patio behind Johnny. The fat face was placid. But Johnny knew this man; knew that Zagin was studying the situation, sizing it, looking for the lead that would give him control of it. Zagin might stumble, but he usually fell on his feet. Johnny grinned mirthlessly.

"Heard something yesterday that brought me in. Mollison says you aim to foreclose the mortgage you bought off Friarson, if he don't rake up a thousand dollars."

"*Ja*! So sad, but we needs the money, Johnny. We pays Friarson so much, almost, for the mortgage. Mollison has the luck. Twenty-one hundreds, Johnny, for only a thousand. But we needs the money, Bill and me."

"How long'll it take you to hand it over?"

"The mortgage? But, Johnny . . . why will you want to know?"

"I want to pay it off for him. Mollison did me a favor, one time, and he's got a bunch of kids. I've got to square this."

Zagin reached into the breast pocket of his

shirt and drew out a cigar. He bit the end from it without taking his eyes from Johnny's blank face. He scratched the match and set the little flame to the cigar end. Johnny met his unwavering stare.

"Johnny!" Zagin said explosively at last. "For why do you come fool the old man—the old friend? *You?* Pay off the mortgage for Mollison? Johnny, Johnny! It is funny! *Ja*!"

"You think I can't? Or think I won't?"

"*Ja*! Both. Something, it is smell funny. I have a nose, Johnny. *Ja*!"

"Do you have to team with Bill Veck to handle this? All right, then! Let's go down to the store and see him."

For a barely perceptible instant, Zagin hesitated, then he nodded. He walked across the patio with Johnny, humming a little German tune. He was the very picture of a benevolent old gentleman. His face might well and fittingly have graced a lager beer sign. Johnny, too, kept his thoughts from showing on his face. But when he swung up on that lifted Heart sorrel which some rider of Whitey Kew's was now lamenting, he untracked the horse and managed to make the saddle without ever taking eyes from Zagin.

Down the street they went, the sorrel's nose almost at Zagin's fat shoulder, until they rounded the partners' store and Zagin unlocked a side door. Johnny had unbuckled the saddlebags and was pushing close behind the fat man when

Zagin stepped inside. Zagin's humming continued placidly. From the little room in which he slept, Bill Veck's voice came, querulous and suspicious. Zagin answered him calmly.

Veck came blinking out of the dark room into the dusky and smelly store. When he made out the face of Zagin's companion, he took a half step backward with a furious oath.

"Nuh! Nuh! Bill," Zagin soothed him. "Maybe so, Johnny gets to be the good friend, yet. Hey, Johnny!"

"Maybe," said Johnny dryly. "Let's amble up to the office, Bill, where we can talk about what I have been telling Zagin. Go on! I wouldn't shoot you from behind, likely."

They sat in the dusky alcove. Johnny, remembering the night he had collected the six hundred dollars in here, and how the killer Hernando had slid up behind him, put his chair against a tall cupboard that partly walled the office from the store proper. He was as alert as a wolf. He watched the pair of scoundrels before him, but he was listening mechanically for the tiniest sound in the store.

"I came in to pay off Mollison's mortgage, Bill. So you can drag it out, and you and Zagin can indorse it paid."

"Huuuuh?" Bill Veck gasped. His murky eyes jerked to Zagin's face. "You—*you* want to pay off Mollison's mortgage?"

"Why, you did understand, now, didn't you? And, me, I'm in a tolerable hurry—as maybe you can figure. So, here's the thousand, all in gold. Bring out the mortgage and indorse it."

He emptied the saddlebag in a heap on the table at his right. Double eagles jingled pleasantly onto the pine. Zagin sucked in his breath. Then he sat calmly, hollow blue eyes squinted against the rising smoke of his cigar, looking at Johnny, not at the gold. But Veck licked his thick lips. He put out a yellow hand, lovingly, to touch the pile. Sweat was twinkling on his forehead.

"Not—so—fast!" Johnny grinned tightly. "Not a nickel do you get, while I have got my health and six-shooter, till I get the mortgage, marked 'Paid,' Bill. Let's have it!"

"I—I don't got it! I—I—I have to get it," Veck mumbled, without taking eyes from the yellow heap that gleamed dully on the table top. "Two or three days—mebbe four—you leave the money, Johnny."

"Thought you two kept your papers here," Johnny scowled suspiciously, looking from one to the other.

"Yesss! Yesss! Most. But thees—thees different. But I get it, I tell you! I give you receipt! I write 'received thousand dollars, for paying Mollison mortgage' and when I get the mortgage . . ."

Johnny stood up and swept the gold from the table, back into the saddlebag. He looked down at Veck's twisted face and shook his head with a mocking smile.

"I'm just a poor cowboy. I *sabe* mortgages, because I have heard about 'em. But receipts without the mortgages, uh-uh!"

Veck was telling the truth. He was sure of that. The greedy eyes that followed every bob of the gold-laden saddlebag could not lie on that subject. Someone else had those mortgages. Veck would have handed over the paper gladly for the privilege of scooping up these double eagles.

"Kesall got the mortgages? Greathouse?" he asked on impulse.

Veck shook his head, still staring fixedly at the saddlebag.

"Johnny," Zagin said abruptly. "You are one fighting son of a dog! *Ja*! Except maybe Nathan Hayes, you are the fightingest little devil in the High Mesa country, *ja*! Now Johnny . . ."

"You said that once before. And I told you I wasn't cut out to be a Ring sheriff. Keep your seats a spell, gentlemen. I'm going out, and I'd hate to be followed. I have a big idea that I'd like to have a drink in the Congress this morning. They ought to be opening up about now.

CHAPTER 15

He opened the side door cautiously and looked out. And there was no sign of his sorrel. He stepped outside, scowling. It might have moved a step or two . . . But it was gone. Clean gone. He ran to the front of the store and looked down the road, now visible for its length in the gray light. The sorrel was not in sight. He looked past the other buildings of the county seat, in the other direction, and there, before the Congress Saloon, tied to the hitch rack, was the horse.

"Oh!" Johnny said softly, very grimly. "Oh, like that, huh?"

He studied the front of the Congress. Someone was inside, he knew. Someone waiting for him to come up to the horse. Who would it be? Some enterprising gunman who had seen him go into the store with Zagin, or a gang of the sort? He moved back from the corner and, at an awkward trot, went along the building-rears, heading for the edge of town, for the house of Felipe Espinosa.

The Espinosas were up, getting ready for breakfast. Felipe grinned tensely at the sight of Johnny, who grinned in reply.

"Felipe," he said humorously, "we are doomed to meet always in the smell of powder smoke, *no es verdad*? Now, I have a little business at the Congress Saloon. Will you jump on that horse of yours and ride by back ways to the house of Judge Biddle? Take these saddlebags and give them to the good Judge? *Gracias, milgracias*! And if I might have two of those *tortillas* . . ."

He disposed of the smoking corn cakes in a few bites. It was good daylight now. He saw Felipe swing up, with the saddlebags before him on the pony; he saw him ride away. Then he crossed the road and moved along the backs of the buildings on that side of the "street," toward the back door of the Congress.

Housewives, Mexican and white, looked curiously at him, but he shambled along, like a cowboy just wakened from drunken sleep under a mesquite bush. He saw no sign of recognition in any face. He came to the Congress's back door and listened. There was a mumbling of voices inside. He looked in and saw three men at the end of the pine bar nearest the door. A bartender stood abreast of them, the bar between. Johnny stepped with infinite caution inside. His gun was in his hand.

He put his weight down, first on one foot, then on the other. For a wonder, the creaky old floor gave no alarm this morning. He watched that group which, in turn, watched through the space above the Congress's swinging doors; watched the corner of the Veck-Zagin store, he knew! The bartender had a towel and a glass in his hands. He was on tiptoe, trying to see over the shoulders of the men at the door. His toweled hand moved mechanically, and it polished the stiff cuff of his white shirt. Under his ropy, waxed mustache, his mouth hung wide open, while he gaped.

"Drop those guns!" Johnny drawled, two yards behind them all.

The result was explosive! The bartender groaned harshly, and there was a ring of shattered glass on the floor. He turned like something moved by a button. Still, his mouth hung open; his watery blue eyes bulged; the towel in his right hand continued to polish his left shirt cuff.

Heinie Eddieford, shotgun in hand, began to turn. Johnny barked at him again. The other two hard-faced, shabby riders, with sweat-stiffened pants clinging to bowed legs, let their Winchesters drop to the floor. Up went their hands. But Eddieford, next to Jink Kesall, the deadliest killer in the High Mesa country, was not minded to surrender. He was beginning to spin about, the shotgun moving upward a trifle, when Johnny quite calmly and without any compunction at all, drove two bullets into his back. Eddieford fell against the swinging doors, slipped sideways, and struck the floor. The shotgun was still gripped in his dead hands.

"The damned fool!" Johnny said, by way of epitaph.

“We—I—Heinie said that a horse thief’s coming up in a minute.” This was the younger of the pair who had held the Winchesters. He was a miniature High Pockets Sill, but without the square chin that kept weakness out of Sill’s face.

“Yeah! I reckon! Never happened to say what the man’s name was, I suppose,” Johnny nodded contemptuously. “You working for Veck and Zagin?”

“Uh—Yeah. But we just started. We—We never done a thing to you, Raff.”

“Oh, so you know who it is! And, so, you knew who it was that Eddieford expected. Well . . . What kind of work have you been doing, that was so honest I oughtn’t to down you?”

“I ain’t done a thing, except carry some letters to Aden, to that big Mex’ politician, Zeke Martinez. Honest! Just toted a big bunch of papers up to Aden for Veck.”

Something moved in Johnny’s mind at the word “papers.” Somebody had those mortgages, for Veck had not been able to produce them. Well! For whom did Veck and Zagin do political jobs? Zeke Martinez! So he nodded blankly.

“If you have just been a messenger boy,” he said contemptuously, “there’s nothing to make by downing you. Go out and untie that horse. Lead him in here, careful! No bobbles, son. You want to remember that my favorite target practice is sitting on a riverbank, shooting out little fishes' eyes."

He looked at the other man, who had stood sullenly quiet the while, a hardcase cowboy, but a stranger. He faced Johnny defiantly. Johnny twirled his gun on the trigger guard for a moment, then half-turned to bark at the bartender.

"Hell of a house! You haven't offered to set 'em up yet!"

He took the bottle and poured a drink left-handed. He gulped it down. The young cowboy led the sorrel inside, pushing back the swinging doors. Johnny had another drink. Nobody had appeared curious about the double shooting. It was still early for drinkers to appear.

"All right!" he grunted. "All of us together, now. To the back door and out!"

He shepherded them to the rear of the place and led the horse outside. The swinging doors in the front slammed back at that moment. Johnny could not make out the identity of the man who stepped in and jostled the body of Heinie Eddieford. But he saw the entering man stumble over Eddieford. Then there was a terrific explosion; the flame from the shotgun's twin barrels making a spurt of orange across the dusk of the barroom corner. Blending with the roar of the shotgun was the affrighted yell of the intruder. He went outside with a crash of his body against the swinging doors.

Johnny grinned.

"Seems that Heinie's as dangerous dead as he was alive—maybe more dangerous!" he told the silent trio with him. "First time he ever shot at a man's front side. Now, I'm going up the line a minute, and I do hope nobody has any ideas about doing a thing but going back inside and—well, just thinking!"

He looked sharply, swiftly, from side to side. Still, nobody in sight. He thought that Greathouse's posse must have included the more dangerous of the county seat's population. Pure accident that Heinie Eddieford should have been left here, to enlist or conscript these two cowboys in the war against him.

He swung up after flashing a look at the saddle cinches. He went trotting, straight out from the back line of the buildings. He wanted a word with Judge Biddle, but as he stepped far enough out to see the road, where it entered the county seat, he saw, straight over his shoulder, the straggling, weary, hunched posse of Monty Greathouse coming in. Johnny's brows climbed. Then he shrugged. "Somebody in that crowd must've had a pet horse," he said to himself. "He caught him, then rounded up the others' horses. Well, *adios*, Mister Sheriff. Be seeing you again, but likely, not in church!"

He gave over thought of seeing Biddle. He leaned a little forward in the borrowed saddle and rammed the hooks to that Heart sorrel. From the posse came a sudden fierce yell. Greathouse's bunch left the road and charged after him, but the sorrel was fresher than their horses. It went at racing gallop, lunging up the hillside that was, here, a slope of the Tortugas. When Johnny rounded to the spot where Ralph and the others waited, lounging comfortably, he saw no more of the posse. He reined in, grinning at them. "And what the devil have you been about, now, Chief Kidney Compound?" Ralph demanded severely, laying down the tattered cards with which he was dealing stud. "Have you no mind for your elders? Putting the white hair of worriment into . . ."

"Never mind! I'd as soon be shot as talked to death. Up, *lobos*, and out of this! Rise up and be ready for the High Society you're heading for. We're heading for the capital. Yessiree! We're going to go mix with the Big Boss, and I don't mean the Governor. Going to go pay a society call on Zeke Martinez, up at Aden!"

CHAPTER 16

They met nobody of importance on the mountain road north from Mesita's outskirts to Aden. From other visits, Johnny knew the lie of Aden, its central plaza, and its crooked, winding streets. He knew the big adobe house of Zeke Martinez, the political boss. He knew, also, Martinez's law office, on the second floor of one of a row of two-story adobes on First Street.

They stopped at Dolores's long, low place on the edge of Aden. Dolores's, famous throughout four hundred square miles for meals, for liquor, for the loveliest dance hall girls, for the wildest fandangos. They put their horses in Dolores's corral and went, four abreast, around the long building to the barroom door.

They had made slight shifts of costume in the corral. They had each unbuckled his shell belt, and their pistols were now rammed into the waistbands of pants or overalls, under the shirts.

In the barroom was the longest bar for many a mile, where freighters, miners, cowboys, cowmen, officialdom, and other unlabeled untalkative gentlemen met on terms of perfect equality. On the white plaster at one end of the backbar case, Gregorio, the half-breed head bartender, had whimsically scrawled, in English, the tally of personal encounters which had occurred in

Dolores's. Appropriately written in red, there was a long list, with dates, names, and final results.

The four had a drink, without exciting any apparent curiosity among other drinkers. They moved next to the tables in an adjoining room. They ate their noon meal and wandered back to the barroom. Johnny found a chair at an empty poker table and propped it against the wall in a corner. He sat with hat brim low over his eyes. Ralph and the others went into the gambling room. Johnny sat motionless, meditating, but watching everybody.

There was a stir at the table at his left. He had casually noticed the entry of the three men in the party, an army officer, with two civilians. Now the officer and one civilian were getting up to move toward the front door. The third man sat comfortably, leaning back with a drink before him. He had a pale, thin, distinguished sort of face, clean shaven except for the long, seal-brown mustaches he affected. Now, Johnny saw, his bright, dark eyes shuttled from one point to another, one rough figure to another, about the barroom. His hands were white, very well-kept. He kept brushing back his curly brown hair, which he wore rather long, from his broad forehead.

"A wonderful picture!" he said pleasantly to Johnny, when he noticed him. "Won't you join me in a drink?"

Johnny hesitated, then nodded and moved to

the other's table. A bartender brought bottle and glass to him.

"You like 'nother, Gov'nor?" he asked the civilian.

Johnny stared hard. So *this* was the Governor! He studied the civilian, who, finding Johnny's eyes boring into him, smiled whimsically.

"You don't mind drinking with a Governor, I hope?"

Johnny grinned and had a single drink. For a while, he and Governor Yager talked idly, about the men in the barroom—where they came from; what they did; and about life in the whole great western country. Without realizing it, Johnny told a great deal about himself and his days of saddle tramping, but instinctively he was silent about his time in the High Mesa country.

"You a lawyer?" he grunted abruptly, stopping short.

"No. I'm not. I'm worse than that," the Governor said humorously. "I'm a novelist! The President happens to be a close friend of mine, and he told me that he'd tried retired army officers and ambitious lawyers in this position, but they weren't satisfactory for various reasons. So he wrote me, I was an American Minister abroad at the time and asked if I wanted to serve here in Aden. I did want to very much. I'd like to write a book about this region, its people, its customs."

"Seems to me I heard you came from Connecticut," Johnny said with a blank face. "You happen to know the Friarsons?"

"Only by name. Old Hartford family. I'm not from Hartford. I'm a product of New Britain, about fifteen miles from Hartford. Oh! Wasn't there a man named Friarson at Mesita? Was he a Hartford Friarson? It seems to me that some rumor drifted to Aden, about his causing trouble in that section; loaning money at usurious interest; riding roughshod over the local authorities; things like that. Probably, he doesn't understand these people. I know that I have had to be very careful in every official move, large and small, affecting them. Their ways are not our ways. Fortunately, some of the educated men, the old-timers, here, have counseled me."

"Zeke Martinez," Johnny nodded, with the barest flicker of his eyes.

"Why—yes! Zeke Martinez for one," the Governor said, staring. "But, how did you know?"

"Whole country knows," Johnny answered evenly. "Like you said, Governor, this High Mesa country is different. News travels fast out here. You said that you don't come from Hartford, but from New Britain. A difference of fifteen whole miles! Out here, if I owned a ranch, it might be fifteen miles from my front door to my front gate. I worked on a Texas outfit, one time, where it was that, and a mile from the front door to the back door!"

"Now, wait a minute! I'm green, and I admit it, but that's too much to swallow. A mile from the front door to the back door?"

"There was a little cañon at the back door. It was a mile going around and coming back across it," Johnny grinned.

But inwardly, he was puzzling. He liked the Governor; he seemed a fine sort of gentleman. But he was so obviously green; so obviously depending on Zeke Martinez for knowledge of local conditions, that Johnny feared to open up.

"That's salty country around Mesita," he remarked with cautious indirectness. "I have been there, and, Governor, when reports come in to you, about anything happening there—well, if they should come to me, I don't think I'd swallow 'em whole. I would sort of explore around the edges and see if everything was exactly the way it was reported . . . Down close to Frontera is the Signal Salt Bed; salt could be got up here, if it was needed . . ."

"You mean more than you're saying," Yager said in a low voice, staring shrewdly at him. "You cowboys always seem to mean more than you say, I've noticed. Is it something about Friarson that you're trying to tell me?"

"More than Friarson," Johnny shrugged. He was uncomfortable. He wondered if he should have opened his mouth. Would a Governor be human? "The whole Ring down there. Starting with Veck and Zagin, the men that run Zeke Martinez's store and who put what men they like into county offices; the killing sheriff and his killing deputies; the whole dirty mess; the headquarters here in Aden, right under your nose. Don't ask me anymore! Just look into things. And then when you are told something, lean back and ask yourself if the man telling it has got a bone in that particular pot!"

He got up. The Governor called him back, but he shook his head and went across the barroom. A heavy-set, ropy-mustached Mexican, wearing a gold marshal's badge, turned at the bar to stare sidelong at him. Johnny pretended not to see the marshal. But when he got outside, instead of going on down the street, he stopped to flatten himself against the wall. With his sheath knife point, he cleaned his nails.

The marshal came quickly through the door and looked up and down the street. When he saw Johnny, he seemed taken aback. He went back inside. Johnny loafed on down the street, then. He knew what he wanted to know, which was that official attention was apt to be paid to him. He wondered why.

Twice, that afternoon, he saw Zeke Martinez. The political boss was a big man, very light of skin, brown-haired, and gray-eyed. He was muscular, and there was a bulge of the blue coat under his left arm to tell of a shoulder-holstered Colt. He had the name of being a salty man, a gunslinger, and had not the slightest notion of fear.

Johnny, loafing in the golden sunlight that sheeted the adobes and stone houses of the capital, kept out of Martinez's sight. For Martinez would recall him from his days with Veck and Zagin. Supper time found the four reassembled. Ralph Naile was grinning. He had won steadily at faro all afternoon, and there was a *baile* on the cards for that night here at Dolores's.

"Fine," Johnny nodded. "You young fellows take in the *baile*, and—I'll be somewhere around."

He sat with them in the barroom after supper, very still, very watchful. Around eight o'clock, the first strains of music came from the dance hall. Ralph, with Dick and Sill, went in, but Johnny stopped at the door. He hung about until the room became fairly crowded. Presently, he saw the tall, broad figure of Zeke Martinez above the shorter Mexicans, across the dance floor. Governor Yager was with Martinez. He nodded and moved away.

He began to wander about the dusky streets. The only light came here and there from the windows and doors of house or store or saloon. Soon, he had the feeling that he was being followed. He stopped and stepped into a doorway. Four men appeared before the dusky opening.

"*Señor*," a husky voice came to Johnny, "I am Manuel Chavez, the marshal. You have a pistol. I command that you hand it over."

"Marshal, huh?" Johnny said. "I knew somebody was trailing me, but I didn't think it was the Law! All right!"

He drew his pistol from his waistband and held it out. "There's my pistol, and it's pointing right at your belly. If you want to try taking it—come on. All of you!"

They hesitated. They were silhouetted vaguely against the light of windows across the narrow street. He was completely sheltered in the dark cavity of the doorway.

"You don't want to! Then I'll tell you this: I'm a Texas man! And I never dodge trouble, but I don't take advantage, either. Let's see . . ."

The forefinger of his left hand came out to stab from one to another, while he counted audibly to four.

"No . . . There are five shells in my pistol. And only four of you. You must go get another man!"

The marshal sputtered. Johnny's pistol muzzle covered them relentlessly, and none seemed to wish to open the ball.

"Git!" Johnny said grimly, at last. "And don't bother me from now on. Git! You don't want a fight!"

He moved forward, and they gave back.

"You be mos' sorree!" the marshal said dignifiedly, in English. But Johnny watched them down the street.

He moved quickly, then. He crossed to the blacksmith shop behind the freight corrals. There he poked about until, from a scrap heap, he fished a piece of iron two feet long, a quarter of an inch thick, and two inches wide. From a freight wagon, he got a coil of lashing rope and cut ten yards from it. Then he went to the back of the two-story block on First Street. Standing on a back second-floor balcony, he looped the rope about a projecting roof beam and scrambled up, then freed the rope.

He crossed the roof softly and made the rope fast to another beam, just above the shuttered window of Zeke Martinez's office. He went down the rope to squat in the deep embrasure. With the iron, he pried and poked until he caught the locking bar and lifted it. A shutter swung back. He lifted the unlocked window and slid over the sill.

"Probably a lot of work for nothing," he muttered. "He'll have 'em in the safe, if he's got 'em here, and opening it's a job past me!"

He closed the window, having drawn the shutter to. There was no sound from the hallway outside the door. He lit the wall lamp and looked about.

It was a room eighteen by twenty. There were pine shelves filled with books around the plastered walls. There was a flat desk, and several pine tables against the walls between bookcases. Too, there was a big iron safe.

The desk, searched, disgorged no mortgages. But there was a letter, in Spanish, from Bill Veck. And the word "*papeles*" occurred often enough to make Johnny sure that it had come to Aden, by the hand of that young cowboy, doubtless, with the mortgages. He searched the whole place grimly. At last, there remained but the safe.

He studied it, tried the old-fashioned handle. But it was beyond him. He shrugged. He would have to try something else. Abruptly, then, he whirled, glared for a moment at the door, then streaked across to blow out the lamp. There were footsteps on the stairway, a mumbling of voices. Then only the sound of footsteps.

Johnny moved to stand beside the door. He heard the rattle of a key in the lock. Then, without further sound, there was a draft on his face.

He poked his pistol forward with left hand; reached out with his right and closed upon a coat. He jerked, and the man was whipped aside. Johnny dug the pistol muzzle more deeply into the captive's belly, spun about, and kicked the door shut.

"Don't you make a move!" he snarled softly. "Not a noise, either!"

"*Muy bien*! Very well!" came the quiet answer, in Spanish.

There was a muttering outside. Then a rattle of the door latch. Johnny leaned closer to his prisoner, digging the pistol muzzle suggestively into him.

"Tell that gang to hightail—that it's all right!" he whispered.

"Chavez! You may go! All is well," the deep voice called. It was a familiar voice. It was Zeke Martinez's.

CHAPTER 17

The footsteps sounded, going away. Johnny waited, listening strainedly. Martinez was as motionless as his captor. When the last faint sound was stilled, Johnny breathed audibly in relief. Martinez made a questioning grunt.

"I was thinking, Martinez," Johnny answered humorously, "what a good deed Marshal Chavez and the rest of your shoulder-strikers did for you."

"So it would seem," Martinez agreed placidly. "Well, Raff, suppose we make ourselves comfortable and see what this is all about. Do you want a light?"

"We have to have one," Johnny decided, after quick thought. "Unless you came up here tonight on something crooked that they know about, they'd think it was funny if you stayed in a dark office. So—yeah! First, we'll bolt the door. Now! We'll move over to the wall and make a light."

He got a match from his hatband and handed it to the politician. While Martinez scratched it and held it with a steady hand to the wick of the oil lamp, Johnny kept his pistol muzzle lightly pressing into Martinez's back. Here was a fit running mate for old Zagin. You might make

Zeke Martinez stumble, but he would strike at you as he fell.

"Now," said Martinez, turning calmly as Johnny backed off a pace, "let's sit down and talk things over. There are things about you I like. Other things that I don't care so much about. But you've grown up since I saw you last, and Zagin thinks you are a pretty tall young man. I'm not so sure."

"What'd you come up here, tonight, for?" Johnny demanded. He watched Martinez move to a big chair behind the flat desk. He moved also, so that Martinez's hands were always in his sight. Martinez took a cigar from his breast pocket and offered it to Johnny, who nodded and caught it.

They put match flames to the cigars, watching each other steadily the while. Martinez blew out a cloud of smoke.

"I came to get a paper that Chavez's son is to take to a certain man for me. It stands to reason that we did *not* come looking for you—else you would be dead, now. But about the other, about your hell-raising at Mesita, Zagin has a very high opinion of you. You could have had the star from Greathouse's vest. Why didn't you take it? Friarson?"

Johnny nodded. He came to sit on the end of the desk with the Colt on his knee. It pointed straight at Martinez, but the political boss seemed not to see it. He looked Johnny straight in the eyes.

"Yeah . . . Friarson," Johnny said. "I made a little promise there by the road, when I came to and found Ed Friarson dead. I promised I'd put lead into every man in that killing posse. I'm doing it, as fast as I can."

"You can't win out, though," Martinez shrugged. "One uneducated cowboy bucking me, why, it's silly, Raff! Be sensible about it. Friarson's dead. You can't bring him back by smoking up Kesall and Eddieford and Greathouse. Neither can you hope to buck all the legal forces I can marshal against you: town, county, even United States authorities. We'll get you and hang you, eventually."

He gestured with his cigar. His expression was friendly, persuasive. It was as if he were talking to a child.

"Now, if you'll agree to be reasonable, I'll give you a note to take back to Zagin. You'll be made chief deputy. Then Greathouse will resign, and you'll be sheriff. That job is worth a net six thousand a year."

"What made you think you could use the Friarson mortgages?" Johnny asked, as if merely curious.

"Friarson mortgages?" Martinez repeated, lifting dark brows. "Why—what do you mean? I, using his mortgages? How?"

It was well done. But then, Martinez had a reputation for acting. He was, without a doubt, the best lawyer in the High Mesa country. He could make a jury laugh or cry as he liked, when his cases got as far as a jury . . . But Johnny was not fooled. He grinned across at Martinez.

"Let's pull 'em out of the safe," he suggested gently. "I came clear up here to Aden to get 'em, and I hate to fall down."

"They're not in the safe! They're not in Aden, so far as I know," Martinez protested, with a note of irritation. "Where they may be, I don't know. As a matter of fact, I don't know anything about them, except that I have heard that Friarson held some mortgages. Now—to jump back: An uneducated cowboy—I don't mean any offense, Raff, but can you even read?"

Blankly, Johnny shook his head. Something was in that shrewd mind, and with his negative head shake, the tiny narrowing of Martinez's eyes told him that his ability to read had something to do with the problem. He lifted his Colt a trifle.

"But I can *write* with this!" he said grimly, indicating his gun, "so, if you want to save the old woman who cleans up the office a big job of mopping you off the floor tomorrow, let's open up the safe and bring out the mortgages."

"Hell! I told you—all right! I'll open it up and show you every paper that's in it, if you have to be satisfied, but I don't know a thing about Friarson's affairs."

He got up and crossed to the safe. Johnny

retained his perch on the desk until the door was opened. Then he crossed the room in his turn to stand slightly behind Martinez. The upper half of the safe was all paper-filled pigeonholes. The lower half was open, with papers stacked upon the safe bottom, and with a canvas sack bulging with money upon them. A pistol, too, an old Remington six-shooter, lay there.

"Now!" Martinez said. "You see the way these pigeon holes are marked? I'll read the labels to you—"

He pattered them off rapidly: deeds to this; abstracts; correspondence in this or that affair. Johnny, behind him and with his face unseen by Martinez, grinned a little as he read the legends on the little tabs. Then he gestured toward the loose papers on the safe bottom. Martinez shook his head and groaned. He squatted before the safe and picked up one string-tied sheaf after another. He pointed to legends on the backs and read them, not always correctly, Johnny noted.

"And that's the lot," Martinez finished, straightening.

"Better put the pistol back, hadn't you?" Johnny asked softly. "It might get you killed. You could almost go on the stage with that slick trick of picking things up and sliding 'em under your coat. But I was watching."

Without sign of being disconcerted, Martinez drew the old Remington from beneath his coat and dropped it on the papers. He reached for the safe door. But Johnny, scowling, checked him. Those mortgages *had* to be in the safe. They *had* to be there! He knew as well as if he had seen them handed over to Martinez, that the saddle tramp had brought them here to Aden.

But when he moved Martinez away and he pawed through the packets of papers himself, reading the endorsements of each, he found nothing like them. He stood, frowning at the political boss's calm face. Martinez shook his head and coughed, moving his feet noisily on the floor. The merest split second of time intervened between a faint squeaking outside, a sound like a stair tread being pressed cautiously down under a climbing foot, and the noise Martinez made.

"It'll be just too bad if somebody tried crowding in on us," Johnny said between his teeth. "Too bad—for you!"

Martinez scowled at that. He turned his head toward the doorway, then tiptoed over to it. With ear pressed against it and face strained as with the concentration of listening, he was almost motionless for thirty seconds while Johnny watched him—watched him but mulled over the puzzle of the mortgages.

"There's nobody coming," Martinez turned to say reassuringly. His whole body pivoted. There was a stubby pistol, doubtless coming from a shoulder holster—suddenly in his hand. He fired at Johnny. Then fired again.

There was a stinging, searing pain in Johnny's left side. He dropped instinctively to a knee, throwing a shot at Martinez's big figure as he dropped. He thumbed back the hammer and fired again. There was a jingle of glass and the *pop!* of an exploding lamp. Then the only light in the big office came from the oil flaming along the floor. There was a slam over on Johnny's right, as of a door opening . . . Only—there was no door there! Johnny knew that office by now as well as he had known the O-Dot house.

"Chavez!" Martinez's voice lifted sharply. "It is Raff! *En el suelo*! On the floor!"

Johnny fired instantly at the sound of his voice. And slammed his fourth, then his fifth, bullet at the scuffing noise of feet, over on the right where a door had opened in a doorless wall. The shot was answered, first by a yell, as to the other men, behind Chavez, then by a pistol, flaming again and again. Lead shredded the floor in front of Johnny, thudded into the flat desk behind him, and even tapped hollowly upon his hat crown. Then came silence, thick, almost throbbing, in that hot room that reeked of powder smoke and burning oil. There was only the dying light of the oil burning upon the floor planks near the wall behind Johnny.

"*Amo*! *Amo*!" called Chavez. Johnny groaned

faintly, artfully, when there came no answer from Martinez to Chavez, for it came to him that Martinez might be wondering if he were dead; might be unwilling to show his position by answering his lieutenant, the marshal. So he made a perfect imitation of the death rattle, ending on a tiny grunt.

"*Amo*! *Amo*!" Chavez cried again. "He dies! He is dead! I killed him. But you? You are not hurt?"

Johnny, moving like a snake across the floor, heard his heavy feet, groping, groping . . . he crawled on. His hand came against the cloth of Martinez's coat. He stiffened, but the flesh under the coat was still, nor did it twitch with the touch of his fingers. He groped for Martinez's pistol. The hand he put out to steady himself rested upon the limp body of the political boss. It touched a bulky packet inside the coat. Then he found the pistol. Chavez was coming closer, making little groaning, whining noises as he came.

Johnny lifted the pistol. It was a double action. He pointed it at Chavez and pulled the trigger. The flame of it blinded him; the roar of it almost deafened him. But he pulled the trigger again and heard the crash of the marshal's heavy body to the floor.

That packet—in Martinez's inside pocket—what would it be? Nothing but papers important to Martinez and meaningless to him? But he snatched at them. Would they be the mortgages, slipped out of the safe by Martinez? He had no idea. He shoved them into the blouse of his shirt. He straightened and leaned across Martinez to draw the door bolt. On the wooden stairs sounded the hammering of running, climbing feet.

Now, if I can slide out through the window . . . he thought.

Then he grinned. He stepped over Martinez and into the dark hallway. He drew the door shut and slid toward the stairhead, keeping close to the wall. He heard the men at the top of the stairs, just ahead of him. They stopped, muttering excitedly among themselves.

"Chavez called! I heard him, and I yelled at the rest of you! That is all I know!" one man said. "Where would he be? In the office of the *patron*? I do not know why he called for us to come. There was shooting after that. But now . . ."

"Let us try the office!" a man grunted. "If he called and we do not answer him . . . the *patron* will have our heads!"

They came on tiptoe, straight toward Johnny. He put his back to the wall. In his left hand was the double action of Martinez. It was either empty or holding only one load. In his right hand, lifted above shoulder level like a club, was his own long-barreled Colt. He held his breath. It seemed impossible for that clump of men to come down this narrow hallway and fail to blunder against him.

One's shoulder brushed the sleeve of his right arm at the elbow. Almost, Johnny smashed downward with the Colt barrel. The man stopped, and Johnny thought that he was puzzling over the matter. But all the others had stopped, too. He dared lift a foot and slide sideways. They went on.

He stole down the hallway to the stairs and went down them almost without sound. At the foot of them, he stopped to listen. A man came running up the dirt walk outside the building. He popped into the doorway, and once more Johnny flattened himself against the wall. The man crossed the little entry. He seemed bound for the stairs and in a hurry.

But his lurching feet brought him to the wall. He stepped on Johnny's feet and was recoiling with a startled exclamation when Johnny struck savagely, twice. Almost silently, he crumpled. Johnny caught him and eased him down. He heard no sound from upstairs. He dared to scratch a match and look at the man's face. It was a Mexican, probably one of the bunch upstairs, coming late.

Johnny slipped outside and went by back ways, without meeting anyone, to Dolores's. The *baile* was still going on in the long room. The noise was audible for two hundred yards. He looked in from the back, standing on tiptoe to look over the shoulders of the *gente*, the people, crowding about all the doors to see their betters dancing. The governor went by, waltzing with a smiling, young-faced, gray-haired American woman. Ralph Naile passed. He looked sideways from the vantage of his towering height to grin at Johnny. He had a pretty girl of Aden in the crook of his thick arm.

Johnny drew back into a corner of the corral and struck a match to look at the papers from Martinez's coat. The mortgages of Edward Friarson . . . and a paper, beautifully written in stiff English, by the hand of some native clerk, he guessed, which seemed to be a conveyance of the several listed mortgages, from Friarson to the firm of Veck and Zagin of Mesita. It bore a date six weeks old, or nearly five weeks before the death of Friarson on the road to Mesita. And it bore Edward Friarson's neat, modest signature at the bottom.

"I'll be damned!" Johnny muttered, staring straight ahead. The match burned his fingers. He dropped it with an oath and stood up, ramming the packet once more into his shirt.

"With Martinez and Chavez cashed in, I reckon nobody in Aden has any reason to look slantways at us," he decided. "I wonder how much I could tell the Governor. He is a pleasant-seeming gentleman, but he wouldn't know what I know about this paper with Ed's name on it. He might figure that it's really what it looks to be."

Slowly, he shook his head. Martinez was crooked as a snake's trail. But for pure, iron nerve, he had been a Man! That was what he had come up to the office for: To put these papers in his safe. Perhaps the forger had only handed them to him tonight. And he could play-act with the mortgages in his very pocket.

"Well! I reckon hightail is our play!" Johnny shrugged to himself. "Even if we could stick and play Old Solid, when they look for the fellow who downed Martinez and Chavez—"

There was a tremendous uproar in the long room of Dolores's. Yells and the sudden stop of the music. A shot. Women's screams. Then, across the open space between the rear of the long house and the corral where Johnny stood staring, High Pockets Sill came sprinting. He was calling Johnny's name pantingly, "Johnny! Johnny! Hell's to pay! Mex' sheriff and a gang got Ralph and Dick Quell! I knew you were out here, saw you look in. I was close to the door—popped out before they saw me."

"What'd they snatch Ralph and Dick for?" Johnny snapped.

"Murder! Chavez, the marshal! That big fellow, Zeke Martinez, that you showed us today—he was leading the sheriff and the posse. He pointed out Ralph—Dick!"

CHAPTER 18

There was no time given to Johnny Raff to decide what he had best do. Out of the dance hall, as if following hard upon Sill's heels, came a tight and venomous knot of figures, showing black with the light behind them. Johnny and Sill stepped back behind the thick adobe post of the corral's gate.

Swift as the movement was, it was caught by sharp eyes in the group of officers. A yell went up, in one voice at first, then made a savage chorus of many voices. And guns flamed. The lead sang by. Johnny grunted to Sill, who made a placid, wordless sound in reply. He trotted off into the darkness of this big, adobe-walled corral and lifted his voice shrilly, fiercely, "Scatter out, boys! Give 'em hell!"

And he blazed away at the press of figures. Yells answered the volley. The dark mass melted as men ran for cover to the right and left. Sill ran back, bearing two Winchesters. He dropped one into Johnny's hand, stepped up to the gate post, and shot the other one empty. Then ran back into the dark.

Johnny squatted where he could highlight the men who moved out there. He fired calmly and carefully. He heard the deep voice of Zeke

Martinez, calm as ever, ordering the attackers to spread out and surround the corral. But Sill was calling softly, before much activity ensued between the corral and the dance hall's back wall. Johnny reloaded the carbine swiftly and sprayed lead along the whole front of the line he held. Then he ran to Sill, who sat his horse, holding the reins of three others: Johnny's and Ralph's and Dick Quell's.

They walked out, each leading a horse, through a gap in the corral wall. They simply walked off into the darkness, leaving yells and scattered shots behind. They made the outskirts of the capital, then turned by narrow, crooked streets back toward its center. Johnny hummed absently to himself.

"Good thing I took a look at the jail today," he said, amusedly. "I looked at it and wondered if ever I'd see the inside. And now I'm hoping to do what I was hoping I'd never do—see the inside of the damn *calabozo*!"

"We'll see the inside or we won't see daylight," Sill grunted calmly. "Won't I hoorah Ralph! He always brags about how big and strong and all he is. Now I'll hoorah him about letting a dozen little Mexes not half his size take him!"

Nobody was on the streets. Down at the corral, there still sounded yells and shooting. Johnny grinned. He wondered if those cautious attackers thought that they still had the pair of them bottled up. Down the street toward the long, low, one-story adobe that housed court and jail, he and Sill pulled in. Johnny dropped the reins and swung to the ground. Sill grunted and followed suit.

They moved quietly, almost flat against the building walls, toward the arched opening that was the street end of a short passage leading to a patio, around which the courtrooms and jail were built. There seemed to be four or five men gathered in the opening. Johnny heard them muttering about the fight in Dolores's as he came nearer. They were all staring that way. Johnny made the last three yards lifting a foot with painful slowness, setting it down, lifting the other foot.

He stood with his back to the corner of the opening, directly behind the talking guards. Sill's elbow brushed his. One of the Mexicans turned and faced Johnny.

"If there were only two more, they are eaten, now!" he said to Johnny, "with forty men there to do the eating."

"*Sí!*" Johnny agreed, stiffening with hand on Colt.

The Mexican turned back to crane his neck. Johnny touched Sill lightly and took a step sideways, into the passage; Sill followed as if pulled by a string; another step. Nobody seemed to notice them. Two more and they were flat against the gray-brown wall, invisible. They worked soundlessly to the patio and looked inside. There was a light showing; the long, narrow rectangle of a partly opened door, across the dirt-floored open square.

They moved quietly toward it. Johnny peered cautiously inside. Sitting on a wide bench with his broad back to the wall, swinging a great ring of iron keys, was a bare-headed Mexican, enormously fat, with a little pearl-handled self-cocker in a shoulder holster under his thick arm.

"I'll take him!" Johnny whispered to Sill. "You watch."

He widened the crack in the door. The turnkey looked up. The tiny eyes, almost hidden in rolls of fat, bulged as Johnny stepped inside with pistol ahead of him. He lifted his arms jerkily as Johnny motioned with his pistol muzzle.

"Where are my two good *amigos*?" Johnny inquired in Spanish. "I hope that you know. For it may be that you have a family?"

"I—I will show, *señor*!" the turnkey muttered. "I—but do not point that pistol at me so. I will show."

He gestured toward the door. Johnny scowled and then stood aside and let the man precede him out. They went with enough noise to keep Sill's head jerking backward toward the entrance, to a heavy wooden door. The turnkey grunted wheezily as he fumbled his keys. Johnny took a step forward and rammed the pistol muzzle into the fat back.

"I say to you, *hombre*, that if those friends of yours do come, you will barely hear them coming!"

The turnkey's movements became instantly agitated. He had the door open with a single thrust and turn of the key. He stepped into a black room. Johnny caught his shoulder and kept the Colt against him. Then he called to Ralph.

"And I was just getting to sleep," Ralph complained. "I thought it would be as well, but if you insist on us going . . ."

Johnny prodded the Mexican toward the voice. There was the clank of a key against the bars. Then a door squeaked rustily.

"Come on, Dick," Ralph grunted. "Do not be waiting to kiss the chambermaid goodbye. Who is this fellow?"

"He takes your place," Johnny grinned. "Pull that pop gun out from under his arm, will you, Ralph?"

They locked the cell door and groped back toward the patio. They were outside and moving toward the street entrance when out of it came the guards. Johnny lifted his voice:

"*Asómate a la ventana,*
Para mi alma no pene—"

“Who is it?” someone called irritably.

“The Governor!” Johnny broke off singing to inform them.

They came up to the other group, which had halted. All were armed, now. Ralph Naile had the turnkey’s little self-cocker. Dick Quell carried Martinez’s.

“I locked the jailer in the cell which held the two Americans,” Johnny informed the Mexicans. “My friends did not desire to stay the night, so they had no more use for the room. Do you wish to stop us now, or will you go look at the jailer? Speak quickly! It is of no import to us!”

“*Cuerpo de Dios*!” a man gasped. “*Los buscaderos*!”

The group gave back. Johnny’s bunch wheeled and, keeping faces towards the guards, backed into the passage. Then the guards opened up with a splattering volley. The four answered it with a couple of shots apiece. Then they ran down the passage, bolted out upon the street, and raced toward their horses. They swung up and spun the horses.

“*Yaaaiiiaaah*!” Ralph Naile yelled thunderously. “Cowboys! Leaving town!”

They raced down the street with a thunder of hoofs that brought men and women running to shuttered windows. They left the capital’s outskirts and swung south. Well past midnight, they left the Mesita road and cut across open country.

With dawn, they holed up on a rocky ledge from which they could watch the country.

Noon came. A dust cloud appeared, far away, in the direction of Aden. Johnny watched it for a long time through his glasses. He shook his head, scowling a little.

"Soldiers," he grunted. "Now . . . what'd they buy into this for? We didn't smack the Governor a bit. Just the local officers. Martinez is the answer. Probably, he went to the Governor and talked him into sending the cavalry after us."

"What the hell!" Ralph Naile cried, lazily rolling from elbows to back and pulling his hat once more over his face, after a look at the dust. "Did you ever see, or hear tell of, soldiers that could find a charcoal elephant in a snowdrift? Do they not always have to take a cowboy, or other civilian, to keep themselves from being blood kin to the Lost Tribes of Israel? Why should we worry about soldiers?"

"You wouldn't worry about nothing," High Pockets Sill grinned slowly. "Like last night. What happened? I'll tell you! The Martinez Monkeys, they got together and says, 'How'll we persuade that big ugly Mick to come out of Dolores's and walk into the jail?' And another'n', he says, 'That's easy! Leave it to me!' He takes him some of that foo-foo powder the gals bathe in, and he takes him a tomatter can and punches holes in the bottom, and he puts the foo-foo into the can and walks along by you. Then he starts for the jail, and you follow him into the cell! Don't be interrupting your betters . . ."

Johnny stared hard at the riders down on the flat, ignoring the howls of Sill, now being systematically rolled under Ralph's huge body. The soldiers seemed to be heading straight for this height. He moved the glasses to the right and left and nodded. Then he turned back to the others.

"Up you come! They have got some trailers, Indians, or Mexicans. They're right on our heels. We'll give 'em a trail to follow. *Por Dios*! by the time they're done tracking us around the Breaks of the Bronco, they'll know heaps and heaps about the High Mesa country that they don't know now!"

They saddled and slipped on down the slope out of sight of the mile-distant cavalry. They rode by canons and arroyos until sure that they were out of sight. Then Johnny led them northeast. They slept out, dry and hungry. But the next forenoon saw them in Guadalupe Grande, where a hundred and fifty miles of railroad made southern terminus.

Here they ate and drifted through the streets from saloon to saloon. They met nobody they knew, but they found that they were famous persons. Men drinking at the bars spoke of the killing of Edward Friarson and Happy Isbell on the road to Mesita, and the tale of Johnny

Raff's one-man war against Veck and Zagin, his killing of Tigre Lopez, Simon Jones, and Heinie Eddieford had grown magnificently in the miles of travel between Mesita and Guadalupe Grande.

"My—stars!" Johnny muttered to Ralph, down at the end of the long bar in the White Crow Saloon on the tracks. "I reckon fond mamas'll make their naughty offsprings go to sleep, by telling 'em that awful gunman Johnny Raff'll get 'em if they ain't good, inside a few years! Did you ever hear tell of such a two-gun, lightning-and-thunder gunfighter as this Johnny Raff? And laying bets about me beating Kesall . . ."

They jogged quietly out, having shown themselves sufficiently to be remembered as four men keeping close together, heavily armed, for Ralph and Dick had new pistols, now, and riding south toward the Bronco's lawless banks. If the soldiers followed as Johnny hoped they would, the officer commanding would certainly identify them.

For four days, they rode through wooded hills that were almost mountains, winding in and out, fording little creeks, through country abandoned to wild animals and wilder cattle and men. At Tecolote Canyon, they were fired upon by a half dozen rifles, but with Johnny's name, yelled from behind the boulders and brush, six hard-faced men came up to shake hands and apologize and wish them luck.

In Hell Gate Arroyo, they rode with a happy-go-lucky young thief past two thousand head of cattle and horses, which bore every brand known for three hundred miles around. And Johnny always found that his name and fame had gone ahead.

But on the morning of the fifth day, when they had passed the Breaks of the Bronco and turned back toward old Fort Lowe, a cowboy of the L-Up-and-Down told them that the soldiers had not tried to penetrate the rustler country. They had turned back to Guadalupe Grande and were on the road to Mesita. He told them, also, that the detachment at Fort Lowe was on the lookout for them.

CHAPTER 19

They went around Fort Lowe and forded the Mesita at a lonely crossing. Johnny led them into the Tortugas north of the county seat. They rode up to the Flying M of Gibb Mollison, and Mrs. Mollison made them very welcome.

"Gibb and Orville Atchley and Walt Jefferies, they got together a couple of days ago," she smiled at Johnny. "Looks like you sort of put heart into Gibb, Johnny. He come home that day after he seen you at Rojo Canon, and he was sitting straight up in the saddle for the first time in a year! He sent word to Kesall like you told him to do, that he couldn't pay a thousand on the mortgages but would try to raise money. And we ain't heard a word about the mortgages, since."

"You won't," Johnny told her, absently. "*I* have got the mortgages. Where are the three of 'em now? You mean they got together and decided to fight the Ring?"

"Yeah. I reckon the bunch of 'em is down on our southwest line right now, exploring around the edges of the Heart. Gibb, he missed a bunch of horses, and I reckon that's going to be their first lick, smacking Whitey Kew. Acting together, they'll give Whitey a considerable bellyache, I bet you!"

“We’ll eat a bite, then, and go see ’em!” Johnny decided.

When they had finished their fried steaks and saleratus-streaked biscuit and inky coffee, they rode toward the line. But before they reached it, they met the dozen men of the three outfits, coming triumphantly back with the Flying M, Flagg, and 77 cows, all bearing burned brands. Mollison and Orville Atchley greeted Johnny enthusiastically. Walt Jefferies of the 77 was not so happy. With him were the two cowboys who had been at the 77 during the trouble with the Ward brothers and with Nathan Hayes. These two grinned friendly enough. Johnny regarded Jefferies whimsically.

“Hell, isn’t it, Walt? You can’t run with the rabbit and bay with the hounds in Mesita County these days. Your only play is to play on our side of the table. For they have got your name in the pot, down at Veck and Zagin’s.”

“That was your doing,” Jefferies shrugged sourly. “But now I’m in it, I’ll stick. It did my soul good, anyhow, to land on that sneaking bushwhacker, Whitey Kew. We rubbed out two of his thieves and two busted down the timber and got away.”

“I want to borrow some of your boys,” Johnny told the trio of owners. “Two from you, Walt, and two Flying M and one from the Flagg. I’m going into Mesita and talk business with the moccasins. Mrs. Mollison says the soldiers left, and Greathouse and Kesall went out with 'em."

At Felipe Espinosa's, on the edge of the county seat, Johnny found only Felipe's *tia*; his ancient, withered, but quite shrewd aunt. She had seen the cavalry ride out, with Greathouse and Kesall. She had not seen them come back.

"I reckon we'll take a chance," Johnny frowned, deciding against more careful scouting. "I want to tell Veck and Zagin about the mortgages I found in Martinez's office up at Aden, and, too, I want to deliver the mortgages to Judge Biddle."

The townsfolk looked neither friendly nor the reverse, as the nine of them rode up the street toward the judge's house. They merely looked with veiled curiosity at the four most famous warriors in the Territory; they looked, too, at the brands on the horses of the supporting cowboys of the Flagg, 77 and Flying M outfits.

Biddle was in the room of his house that he used as an office. To him, while the rest of the riders watched the street, Johnny told his tale and delivered the mortgages.

"Johnny, I don't know what to say," Biddle frowned, at the end, staring down at the sheaf of papers on his knee. "I can't see the end of this. Except . . ."

"I know what you mean," Johnny nodded. "I'm in so deep that I'll never climb out, no matter what happens. I can do the job I set out to do and see it net me nothing. And . . ."

"And that loses you a good deal, doesn't it, Johnny? Loses you—Elenore Lovess?" the judge asked softly.

"No . . . No. You can't lose what you never had. I reckon I've done all the losing in that line that I can: I had a notion, a dim sort of hope, a long time ago. I lost that. But I never had a chance. So I can't lose my chance. I'm not a bit keen about dying, even so. I found that out on the 77 when I was kicking at the end of Nathan Hayes's saddle rope. Well! *No es importe*! I'm doing something for the good of the country. If I can keep out of handcuffs for a while longer, I'll do more. And then, if I'm still alive, I'll hightail. Mexico."

He went out to the others, sitting their horses in the street, watching the quiet front of the Veck and Zagin store up the line, watching, too, the front of the Congress Saloon. He swung up and, with a grin, moved toward the partners' store.

They breached the long adobe wall that lay between store and warehouse. And, without warning, it suddenly flamed gunfire. A Flying M cowboy fell sideways against Johnny with a hole in his forehead. The rider of the Flagg crumpled over his saddlehorn, and his slipping heel scratched his horse, which promptly ran away and began to buck in front of the store, unseating its dead rider.

Johnny whirled his horse. Up on its hind legs, the black reared. Johnny rammed in the hooks and sent the horse at the wall. The crackle of firing ran along it. Ralph Naile yelled ferociously and followed Johnny. The others, hardly slower, humped low in the saddles and charged after.

The black lifted himself and cleared the barrier. He came down on a man, who screamed horribly. Greathouse, with face distorted, leaped backward and fired three shots almost into Johnny's face, but missed. Johnny shot at him as the black landed. But whether he hit him, or a bullet from one of the others, now up against the wall on the other side and shooting over it, killed the sheriff, he had no idea.

There were seven or eight men left. They ran, diving into the *acequia*, the ditch that watered the orchard here. They crawled along the ditch, with the fire from the wall spurring them on. By the time Johnny reached the *acequia*, Greathouse's men had gotten to a wing of the store. He snapped a half dozen shots in that direction, then turned back. Ralph Naile and Dick Quell were over the wall in the orchard. They had a prisoner.

"Well!" Johnny said grimly, recognizing the hardcase cowboy he had captured once before, in the Congress the day he killed Heinie Eddieford. "Seems that you can't take good advice. I thought I told you to pick up your feet the last time I saw you. But you stuck to bushwhacking."

“ ’T was him got the Flying M boy,” Ralph said, with thumb moving suggestively at the hammer of his pistol. “Sure it was! I saw that hat of his, and he let drive, first shot, before I’d time to yell, and he hit the Flying M boy.”

“Go on! Shoot and be damned,” the cowboy snarled. He was white-faced, and his right arm, upon which Johnny’s horse had landed, dangled helplessly. “Soon be shot as talked to death, anyhow. Nobody’s running *me* nowhere!”

“Now, what?” Dick Quell grunted, staring at the store’s sinisterly quiet walls. “Can we bust that place?”

From far away, from outside of Mesita, Johnny thought, there sounded, faint but clear, the notes of a cavalry bugle.

“Soldiers coming back . . . And we got Greathouse and . . .” he moved the black to stare down at the other dead man, “Vann Prickett. Well! Vann always did want to be an officer and pack a big pistol and shoot people. And now he’s a dead hero . . . Hightail! We can’t fight the damn army, but we *can* take our two boys!”

There seemed to be no more fighting heart in Mesita. Johnny led his little band back to the street and up it. They delivered a volley that smashed windows in the front of the Veck and Zagin store; sent another to crash into the Congress Saloon, but there was no return fire.

“Come on!” Johnny said disgustedly. “Let’s get our two that they bushwhacked!”

He and Ralph Naile leaned to pick up the fallen Flagg cowboy. Sill and Dick Quell similarly lifted the man from the Flying M. They loaded the bodies on the men’s own horses and went at a walk, in a tight group, out of a sullen town.

From a hilltop, they watched the cavalry come into Mesita and marked the activity, the running to and fro on the street. But the cavalry made no move to follow them, so Johnny led them on to a quiet canon, where they buried their dead under a juniper. They rode on to the Flying M that night.

CHAPTER 20

"I'm going over to the Spear," Johnny told Mollison at breakfast time. "Lovess is going to have his chance to side with us. We need him, and I think he needs us."

"Yeah?" Mollison snarled. "Nathan Hayes rode by yesterday, after you'd hit for town, and Atchley and Jefferies was gone. He was full of talk, Hayes was. Yeah! The Spear is going to bear down heavy, he says. And who do you think it aims to lean onto heaviest? Me and the 77 and the Flagg! Hayes says the Spear's missing heaps of stuff. Him and Lovess, they don't believe the Heart and the D-Bar are on the rustle. So that leaves us. And he gave me warning: I'd better not mix with the Flagg or the 77. I'd better tend to my own knitting, Hayes says, and pray. You'll have no luck at the Spear."

"Got to try, anyhow," Johnny shrugged. "Yeah. Got to."

They did not need to ride to the Spear, as it happened. For not five miles up the Spear-Mesita road, they met Hugh Lovess, with Elenore and her two *vaqueros*. Johnny lifted his hand in the ancient peace sign of the Indian, palm outward. For Lovess and his party had pulled in, fifty yards away, to stare.

They jogged on, then, both parties, and pulled in to look curiously at one another. Johnny ignored Elenore after the briefest of colorless nods. She sat with gauntleted hands folded on her saddlehorn, drawing dark brows down over a straight nose, half frowning. Lovess lowered down at Johnny.

"Well!" he said grimly. "Quite a hell raiser you turned out to be, Raff! Now you got Greathouse and Vann Prickett and Bill Veck, huh? How long you think you'll last?"

"Veck?" Johnny cried. "Got Veck? Ah . . . you're crazy! We got Greathouse and Prickett, all right, when they bushwhacked us from behind the orchard wall. But Veck—I haven't seen him since I was talking to him about Ed Friarson's bunch of mortgages, that Kesall stole from the O-Dot, and Veck and Zagin and Martinez were trying to collect on their own. That was ten days ago. Somebody's been hurrahing you, Lovess."

Lovess's grim face twisted. Surprise and indignation showed upon it. Johnny understood: The cattle king was used to being treated with much deference, and to be talked to as an equal by a man he had once hired, to be told contemptuously that he didn't know what he was talking about—Lovess was on the edge of exploding. Johnny beat him to it.

"But that's not the point, this morning! I was headed for the Spear to talk to you about the

way things have been going. You're a big man in this country. One way and another, you've come to be the biggest cowman. The way I figure it, you're too big, now, to be able to sit on the fence. I think you know that, too. Hayes going to Gibb Mollison yesterday with that cock-and-bull yarn about rustling proves it. It looks like you've slid off the fence, down onto the Martinez side, and all I want to know is that much: Have you, or not?"

"Listen, you! You've done a few killings, and it has swelled your fool kid head all up!" Lovess snarled. He made a shaky gesture with his clenched right hand. His dark face was darker with angry blood. "To hear you yap, you'd think *you* was running the country. Well, you're going to get a smack in the nose that'll wind you up like a ball of string! The Spear is my outfit, and anybody that thinks he can tell Hugh Lovess what to do—I don't give a damn who he is!—is going to get tromped on. You get to hell on down the road, and don't let me catch you on the Spear! Stay clean away from it! You . . ."

"There's no law to keep you from doing as you please," Johnny said thoughtfully. "So long as you're willing to pay for the pleasure. But don't ever think that you won't pay, Lovess. Swelled up, am I? Well, you stop at the first looking glass you come to . . . you'll see somebody that really is swelled up. But you'll have the air let out of you; you'll look exactly like one of those toy balloons. I'm warning you, now: You won't do anything against us, if you don't do anything for us, the way you ought to!"

"I'll do as I damn please!" Lovess yelled furiously and beat his saddlehorn with a huge fist. "And I'm telling you, Johnny Raff, that you're going to run up against trouble with a big T!"

"If the Spear has anything to do with that trouble of mine," Johnny assured him grimly, looking the big man levelly in the eyes, "it's going to be the hardest year that you ever saw. It'll cost you more than you'll want to pay. If you can't see the proper side to get on, maybe you can be shown! I'll do my best to show you!"

Lovess made a snarling, contemptuous sound. He snatched up his reins and rode past Johnny. The *vaqueros* trailed him. Elenore followed, too, but only for a few yards. Then she whirled her horse and came back to where Johnny still sat staring after Lovess. She reined in at his stirrup and met his calm stare with angry eyes. "You have swelled up a lot, Johnny Raff! But Nate Hayes—"

"I know," Johnny nodded placidly. "He's going to shoot on sight, so that makes it mutual. He's going to shoot, but about the other—what I had to tell your father—I wish you'd help me make him get a new idea into that thick head of his. This is war! If we beat the Martinez Ring, this High Mesa country's going to be a sight better place for everybody. He ought to see that. He ought to be helping us by coming down hard on Whitey Kew and Joe Downer and the others that play with Zagin and the rest of the thieves. If he can't see it by himself, I'm going to have to help him."

"Do you think . . ." she stopped to look him contemptuously in the face ". . . that Hugh Lovess or Nathan Hayes, grown men both, are apt to worry about *you?*"

Johnny shrugged and kept his calm expression with an effort. "Hugh Lovess won't have to worry about me, so far as his hide's concerned, for I'm not a forgetting soul, Elenore. I owe you my neck, since that day at the 77. I'll pay that debt one day. But so far as Nathan Hayes is concerned . . ."

She waited. Her face was puzzled, watchful, now, rather than angry.

"Well?" she prompted him. "What about Nathan Hayes?"

"It's different with him," Johnny told her softly. "If I stood in Hayes's boots, I'd be doing considerable worrying. He horned into my business and tried to rub me out for no reason at all. He interfered when he knew well enough that I was recovering stolen horses from a bunch of thieves. He decided to help out Veck and Zagin and Martinez and the Wards by lynching me. For no reason at all! All right! I've decided that this country is not big enough for both of us. So either Nathan Hayes buys a trunk, or I kill him. I don't know what turned him against me."

"You don't?" she interrupted, incredulity in her tone. "You really don't know, Johnny?"

"I don't! But since it's gone this far, what it was makes no difference. He leaves the country, or I kill him!"

She stared at him until he frowned.

"What's the matter?" he demanded. "What are you staring at me for?"

"I swear, I don't know what to make of you," she said helplessly. "In more than one way . . . you're bent that you'll hang and rattle, and try to smash Martinez and Zagin and Kesall, and Hayes, and make Hugh Lovess side with you?"

"I'll hang and rattle," he nodded stubbornly. "I wish you could see it my way, Elenore. I wish you could."

"I see a lot of things," she told him. Her tone was careless. "But I don't see you slapping leather with Kesall or Hayes and coming out on top, and least of all do I see you making Hugh Lovess buy into this mess on your side."

He looked into the pretty face for a long half minute, studying it feature by feature with painful intensity, but there was nothing in her expression, nothing that he could find, to encourage him to go on. He shrugged.

"Well," he said, "in spite of that, I'll go on as

long as I can. If I'm not stopped, I'll do what I've promised myself. After that, I'll cross into Mexico, and I know well enough that, by that time, I'll have so much against me I'll never be able to come back until I've got a long, snow-white beard to hide behind."

"If you went now," she told him slowly, and rather as if thinking aloud, "I imagine that most of this hell you've raised would die down in a year or two. Then you could come back. Even to a job on the Spear."

He shook his head, smiling twistedly. She looked at him. Then, " 'Bye, Crusader!" she said, hardly above a whisper. "You haven't got a lick of sense, and you're blind as a bat, but . . ."

She whirled her horse and threw it forward into a racing gallop. Johnny watched her go in the wake of Lovess and the *vaqueros*. Once, he thought that she looked back, but before he could do more than straighten in the saddle, she had turned her face to the front again and disappeared around a bend.

Johnny turned to the silent trio behind him. He felt suddenly very tired.

"And now, wither away, Chief Nitwit?" Ralph Naile demanded, keeping his eyes trained upon the high tops of the cottonwoods beyond Johnny.

"Bravo," Johnny shrugged indifferently. "I feel like going on a spree, and we'll be safe enough in Bravo."

He led them, without speaking ten words in twenty miles, to the *plazita* that sprawled beside the Rio Mesita, southeast of the Flagg range. The population was Mexican, for the most part, except for a couple of storekeepers and a few hangers-on at Quinn Evans's Crystal Saloon.

It was at the Crystal that Johnny established headquarters. The huge, taciturn Evans made the four of them welcome with a colorless sort of courtesy. He was not a man to take sides.

But it was from Evans that Johnny learned how Veck had died: A bullet of that last volley which they had fired into the store had glanced from a wall and ricocheted into the little office enclosure. It had struck Veck in the face, and the half-breed had died instantly. Three murder warrants were out for all the party—for Veck's death and Prickett's and Greathouse's.

"And Kenneth Vardaman is sheriff," Evans said tonelessly. "No, I never heard why Jink Kesall was passed up. No, I don't know how he feels about it. No, I don't know if Vardaman has tried to arrest the cowboys that was in the fight with you men." And that was all that Johnny could pry out of the cautious Evans!

For three days, they drank and played cards and danced in the long dirt-floored room behind the Crystal, where the Mexicans gave their *bailes*. Johnny drank as he had never drunk in his life before. He never got beyond the ability to walk, but neither was he ever sober. The pretty, brown-skinned girls who snuggled close to him and looked adoringly at him during the dances were no more than vague shapes to him.

Nothing seemed of any use or value. He had done pretty much what he had promised himself to do, to pay for the murder of Friarson. Every man of that murder posse was dead, with the exception of Jink Kesall. But Martinez still rode the crest up at Aden. Zagin was more powerful than ever, with the death of Bill Veck. Stealing and killing still went on around Mesita. The 77, the Flagg, the Flying M—all were losing stock. Word came to Bravo that on the same morning, a 77 and a Flagg cowboy had been found dead on the range, shot in the back. And how could *he* hope to stop it all, pull Martinez and Zagin down? And if he did, what would it matter?

"What did she mean?" he asked himself dully, over and over, as he drank. "She said that I could probably come back later. To a job on the Spear. Did she mean that I could come back and have a chance with her?"

But there was no answer to that. So he kept the whiskey at a certain level in him. He was not too drunk to know what was going on about him, but he was drunk enough not to care greatly. Then a stranger appeared in the Crystal. Johnny saw him talking to Evans and looked without interest at the grinning cowboy. Then, after some minutes,

Evans shrugged his huge shoulders, and the cowboy came over to where Johnny sat with one booted leg on the table before him, a quart and a tin cup within reach. He sat down and grinned at Johnny.

"If you don't take that happy look away from me," Johnny said slowly, thickly, "I will take out my knife and—and operate! And you never will, no more, grin like that!"

The grin widened. The stranger was a stocky, middle-sized figure, with wide, staring, china-blue eyes. His gun swung awkwardly high on the right side.

"I rode over to hook up with you, friend," he said. "I was to Mesita, and that new sheriff, he was feeling his oats. So, when I made holes in the Congress's ceiling, Vardaman ran me out of town and chased me ten miles. I'm from way up in Idaho. I love excitement, and they do say you can't ride with Johnny Raff and not have plenty. So I want to ride with you."

"Don't need you," Johnny said flatly.

Through the open door, he saw a buckboard pull up before the saloon. A slender, erect young man got down. He was dusty, but there was marked neatness about him, despite the signs of the road. He stood on the plank sidewalk, framed by the door opening, looking up and down. The buckboard drew away from him. He seemed to decide to come inside.

Everyone in the place looked at him curiously. Of Johnny's bunch, he was the only one in the Crystal. Ralph and the others were out in town somewhere. But there were some cowboys from distant outfits, in for a spree. And there were several Mexicans. The newcomer walked up to the bar. He was no cowboy. He walked, shoulders back, with a brisk slapping of heels on the sagging floor. He said something to Evans and the saloonkeeper, after a long stare, jerked a thumb toward Johnny. The young man came over.

"Raff?" he inquired stiffly—and with evidence of distaste. "I'd like to talk to you for a while."

"Go ahead!" Johnny invited him with a large gesture. He poured another drink and held the bottle up hospitably.

"No, thanks! And if you'll take a suggestion, it might be better to postpone that one until we are done talking. You seem to have had plenty, already."

" 'S 'at so?" Johnny drawled. "Preacher? Ask Evans to give you five dollars as you go out. Charge it to me. Building a church, huh? Well . . . this country could stand a few. Fine work. Tell Evans to give you ten dollars. Now, go away. You have a—a—bad 'fect on me. Cost me too much. 'Bye!"

"I'm not a preacher!" the young man snapped. His smooth face was red and angry. "I'm—does this fellow have to stay here and listen? I can't talk before him."

"Say!" the grinning cowboy grunted—and his grin vanished. He got up, staring blue eyes abruptly hard and cold and opaque. "Who the hell you think you are, anyhow! The Epistle Paul, maybe? My name's Merle Jackson. I hail from Idaho, and no lily-fingered dude—"

Johnny slipped his foot from the table, caught its edge in the arch of his boot sole, and pushed it crashing against Jackson. The cowboy sat down on the floor with the table in his lap.

"You—bother me!" Johnny said querulously. "First 'twas your damn happy grin. Now, you talk too much. Tell Evans to give you a drink and charge it to me. But drink it up at the far end of the bar, to do me a favor. Now, Mister, sit down."

The muttering Jackson moved over to the bar. Johnny looked thoughtfully at the stranger, who glanced at the chair but decided not to take it.

"I'm Lieutenant Serrells of the Governor's staff," he said quickly, in a low voice. "I was ordered to bring a message to you. I've been to Mesita and—the Governor sends this message:

" 'I have just learned that the cowboy to whom I talked in Dolores's is Johnny Raff, for whom several warrants have been issued. I ask Johnny Raff to come to Aden, quietly; to come to me for a conference. It may save much bloodshed. It may even bring peace to the Mesita region.' "

Johnny blinked at the young officer. Slowly, then, he shook his head. Lieutenant Serrells's smooth face tightened disapprovingly. It was evident, indeed, that this errand was not to the taste of the dapper young man.

"Don't be a fool!" he exploded. "This is the Governor talking! To—to—*you!*"

"Yeah. So I gathered. And the answer, sonny, is 'no'! I will not come to Aden. But I *will* meet the Governor—anywhere outside of that den of rattlers. And talk to him about anything he picks for the conversation."

"I'll not take such a message back to him! Not from a—a drunken man! I'll stay until tomorrow morning. You might try sobering up and thinking this over. It's serious!"

"Son!" Johnny grinned, "you have no real idea of how serious it is. Trouble with you young military fellows is, after the taxpayer sends you to college, you get a notion that you're set on a little pinnacle away up above the folks that paid for your education. Hell! If it wasn't for us paying the bills, you'd be swinging a pick, likely. Don't get notions, son, and remember, this business is between the Governor and me. You have got my answer. You take it to Governor Yager the way I gave it!"

CHAPTER 21

He watched the young officer go with stiff, indignant back up to the end of the bar, beyond Merle Jackson of Idaho. He watched Serrells order his drink and saw how Jackson watched, too. Frowning a little, Johnny saw the Idaho man pull his pistol furtively; point it downward at the floor . . .

Johnny got up, then. He went toward them. He was ten feet away when Jackson heard him coming and looked that way. The china-blue eyes held that same cold, hard opacity that had marked them when Serrells crossed him at the table.

"None of that, Jackson!" Johnny drawled. "He's a visitor."

"No?" Jackson said. Grinning good nature vanished from him, like a mask stripped off. Killer, he looked; killer, he doubtless was. Something moved in Johnny's liquor-hazed head. Something odd, furtive, sinister, that had been felt but dismissed, as he had watched the conference between Jackson and Evans.

"I made a mistake," Johnny told himself as Jackson's hand came up, lifting the Colt. "I underrated the fellow."

It seemed hopeless, trying to draw to beat the shot of a man who had his gun out and pointing. The quick flame of killer triumph was in the staring blue eyes when Johnny's left hand dropped the cigarette that he was putting into his mouth, seized his hat brim, and sailed the hat at Jackson.

He was pulling at the same time. But, intent as he was on his draw, he heard Jackson's shot. He paid no attention to it. If it hit, it hit. He was concentrating on pulling his gun. It came out, cocked. Instinctively, rather than consciously, Johnny leveled it and let the hammer go.

Serrells had hurled himself backward, out of range. So had the other drinkers. Jackson's head jerked as Johnny's bullet caught him in the stomach. He held onto the bar with his left hand and fired again. This shot was wilder than the one the sailing hat had made a miss. Johnny's head was ice-cold now. He thumbed back the hammer and shot the gunman between the eyes. Then he turned slowly to look at Quinn Evans. Upon the heavy, stolid face of the saloonkeeper, twinkling beads of sweat appeared as he met Johnny's level, probing stare.

"I didn't think you'd try that with me, Evans . . ." he said slowly. "I never *trusted* you, but still I didn't think you'd dare!"

Evans's hands came up with speed amazing for such a fat and clumsy seeming man. Johnny's Colt twisted as the bar-shotgun appeared. But from the back of the saloon, there was a double roar of pistol fire. Evans fell sideways, taking the shotgun with him. Up the saloon came Ralph and Dick Quell, elbow to elbow, guns out, with High Pockets just behind.

"It's all right," Johnny told them calmly. He ejected the exploded shells from his Colt and reloaded from his belt. "Zagin sent over a gladiator to collect my scalp. Evans was in on the deal. And now—Evans is not!"

He found Serrells standing in a corner, very white of face. Slowly, sardonically, a corner of Johnny's hard mouth climbed.

"You see," he addressed the lieutenant, "I'm fairly sober. So you really don't need to wait to be sure that my head was clear a while ago."

"He—he was going to kill me. I have to thank you."

"No," Johnny disagreed, tolerantly, "he wasn't after you at all. He was just going to use you to work me up to where he could try what he did. Killing, with that fellow, was just a job of work. He went at killing a man the same as he'd go about putting up a windmill. Just a mechanical kind of job, and, same as for all of us gunfighters, there came a time when he had to lose."

He went on out, then, with the three at his back. Down at the long adobe house of Jesus Francisco Tiscareno, he sat upon a bench and stared moodily across the street. Ralph and the others made themselves comfortable around him. Beatriz, fifteen years old, barefoot, pretty, in her estimation already a woman, came out of the house and toward Johnny. Ralph grinned and reached out a long arm to catch her.

"No, no, no!" she cried, slapping his hand down. "You are big of body, but he is big of head, Ralph. I have something to say to Juancito. I must not be troubled by you. Juancito . . . I must tell you something."

She put a hand upon his shoulder, leaning to him until her cheek brushed his. Johnny still stared blindly straight ahead.

"One from the Spear is here, to speak to you. The *vaquero* Fierro. He brings word. He is now behind our corral."

Johnny's head snapped around. He came to his feet in a single movement. Beatriz stared curiously. He went past her.

"I'll be back pretty soon," he told Ralph and the others.

Fierro, younger of the bodyguards of Elenore Lovess, squatted behind the corral. He looked up at Johnny, flipped away his cigarette, and stood up.

"I could not safely come into the town to hunt you," he said. "There are too many eyes, everywhere, *la señorita* says."

"*La señorita*!" Johnny said incredulously, though that was what he had hoped for. "Is this word from—from her?"

"From her," Fierro nodded. "And without the knowledge of her father—or of Hayes. She ordered me to learn where you were and give this word to you and to none other: She says that she has talked much to her father, since the day we met you upon the road. Don Hugh is a stubborn man, as you know, Juancito, but he listens to her as to none other. And she has asked him to do as you asked. Not altogether because you asked, but because it is the better way, not to fight for those *ladrones*, those thieves, of Mesita. But Hayes pulls Don Hugh the other way, so, she asks you to come and talk with her; and then to talk with Don Hugh, standing beside her. She will be, tomorrow, at the ford of the Rio Vaca north of the O-Dot house, on the Spear bank of the Vaca. You will come alone, so that Hayes will not be alarmed. Four might be noticed. I am to say if you will come."

"Unless my horse dies under me!" Johnny said simply.

"*Bien*! Then I ride. *Hasta la vista*, Juancito!"

Johnny went back to the house. Beatriz looked inquisitively at him. Ralph Naile whistled softly and liquidly.

"All right, you mesquite hoppers! All that's young enough to straddle a horse, up you come. We're hitting for the O-Dot. Friarson's place, you know. Fast."

"You are going?" Beatriz asked Johnny softly

when he was pulling cinches near the others in the corral.

"Yes. We go. Something was wrong, *dulcita*, when we came to Bravo. Wrong today, until . . . Well, all is well now, so we ride once more, with shoulders back, feeling like men."

"It is a girl!" she blazed. "You go to a girl. And for three days and three nights I look at you, I smile at you, and you—you look not at, but through and past me. What is this girl? Will she stand beside you as I would; love you, fight for you, lie for you, as I would?"

Johnny gaped at her, turning with the end of the latigo dangling in his hand. As she had said, he had looked through or past her, and now, it seemed, he had stepped on her toes.

"You are very good," he told her slowly. "At another time, when there is not so much on my mind, my eyes may be different. But now—I go to fight."

"They say that you will go to Mexico, soon—that you *must* go, soon, with all the officers following like wolves, as they are. Juancito, when that time comes, will you take me with you? Or, if you cannot take me, send me word of where you are. I will come!"

"You will hear from me," Johnny promised evasively.

"Come on, Romeo!" Ralph yelled. "You said we ride fast."

They went at a long trot, due north from Bravo, then—safely out of sight of the *plazita*—turned west. They ate black beans and tortillas with a herder of Nacho Howze, well after dark that night. The goat herder was greatly honored to entertain such famous ones. Johnny took from Ralph Naile the little self-cocker revolver of the Aden turnkey and presented it to the Mexican, making a changeless friend of that simple soul.

They ate goat meat and beans with him before dawn. Then Johnny sent Dick Quell angling off to the Flying M, to learn from Gibb Mollison what was going on. He and Ralph and Sill trotted on toward the O-Dot house. They reached it in midmorning. The low stone house was like a tomb. There were many bootprints in the dust around it and on the floor of the house itself. It brought back vividly the picture of Edward Friarson. Johnny shook his head and went back outside.

"Ralph, you two will stick here. I'm going to scout up the Spear ford, clear up the Spear house, maybe. So if I'm not back before tomorrow night, don't bother. There's grub in the little cave in that juniper thicket yonder. I cached it there the last time I was here."

"You're a damned fool!" was Ralph Naile's opinion. "With the Spear just pining to lift your scalp, you will go sashaying off on your own. Why don't we all scout up that way?"

“Because, my darling, one man makes less than one-third the target three men’d make. You never were built for this country, anyway. When we ride down an arroyo, your blame head’s sticking up above the mountains. Anyway, I don’t need company.”

“Johnny! Something about this is damn funny. Now, do you not wish to be telling your big, handsome, clever Uncle Ralph what’s troubling you? What was it the *vaquero* said to you so confidingly, out beyond the corral in Bravo? You were miles deep and to the neck in sorrow till you met that *vaquero*. And since then, you’ve disgraced the lot of us, acting the ten-year-old. I swear, Johnny, you giggle like a schoolgirl. Johnny . . . are you riding to—meet that girl? Tell your Uncle Ralph!”

“I haven’t got an Uncle Ralph!” Johnny grinned. “The only Ralph I know is a long-coupled, long-nosed Irish jigger that’s due to be hung or shot, and he’s so disrespectable I wouldn’t mention knowing him around nice people. I’ll be back when you see me coming. Keep the coffee pot on!”

He jogged on uphill through spicy juniper and cedar, over the well-remembered trail to the ford. His eyes were alert, instinctively. But his mind was not upon the things before him. Why should Elenore trouble herself so much about his “crusading,” as she called it? There was only one explanation, but it was one he could hardly believe.

"She let me hang around on the Spear last year, picking and fetching for her, and she let me think that the Big Boss's daughter *could* look at a saddle tramp . . . Then, she was *so* surprised when the saddle tramp kissed her that day on Black Ridge. Never had she dreamed of such a thing! And the impudence of the business, too . . . And now . . ."

He could not see a satisfactory ending to his problems. He ticked off the warrants against him with tap of finger on his saddlehorn; they charged him with the murders of Annear, Tigre Lopez, Hernando, Greathouse, Prickett, and Bill Veck. Doubtless, up at Aden, he had been indicted for killing the marshal, Chavez. And if these charges were not enough, they could and would add Heinie Eddieford, Simon Jones, Oliver Ward, the hardcase *vaquero* at the 77; the other Ward hand, Ollitt—whom Dick Quell had downed; Quinn Evans; even the Idaho killer, Jackson.

No matter what Elenore might persuade Hugh Lovess to do, there remained this legal angle. Even if the inconceivable came true, even if she admitted that she felt toward him as he had always felt toward her . . .

He shook his head gloomily. And yet, he could not be downcast altogether. It was much, even to see her again. He came near one o'clock, down the southern bank of the Rio Vaca toward the ford. He rode neither carefully nor carelessly. For it was possible that others might be in the neighborhood, though he did not expect anyone up here.

From behind a clump of bushes, he looked down at the ford. The sound of flowing water over the stones was all that he could hear. Of the girl, there was no sign. He sat studying the Spear bank, fifty yards from his hiding place, then pressed his knees against his horse and rode down the slope toward the water. He was at the bank when the *vaquero* Fierro rode out into the trail on the stream's far side.

CHAPTER 22

"Come over, Juancito!" Fierro called, beckoning.

Johnny splashed into the water and across. Fierro, with a leg crooked comfortably about his saddlehorn, smoked his cigarette and waited. Johnny pulled in at Fierro's stirrup.

"She waits farther up," Fierro said. "At Snake Creek."

What it was about the *vaquero* that he suddenly distrusted, Johnny could not say, but his days on the dodge had made him as instinctively watchful, suspicious, as any scarred old *lobo*. Something about Fierro, the flicker of his narrow eyes, the set of his mouth, warned Johnny, then.

But in the flash of time needed to consider this, a rope whirred with a dry whistling sound, out of the thicket behind him. Neatly, it dropped over his arms, pinning them to his sides. Fierro grinned fiercely and leaned toward Johnny with hands coming up to snatch at him.

"*Hijo de la perra*!" Johnny snarled at the *vaquero*.

His hand had gone mechanically to Colt butt, with the first whir of the dropping loop. He twisted sideways, strained against the tightening manila. The gun would not come out—he could not lift his elbow high enough. But he could lean far sideways in the saddle, far enough to fire and fire again, through the toe of the holster. Fierro's sudden grin looked like a skull's. His hands twitched. He shivered violently.

"*Muerto*!" he screamed—and collapsed in his saddle.

The rope jerked, and Johnny's subsequent shots—for he emptied the six-shooter through the holster's end—splattered into the thick leaves beyond Fierro's huddled body. Out of the brush came riders. Johnny straightened to look grimly at them. Kenneth Vardaman, a one-cow rancher, Veck and Zagin henchman, a slow-thinking, bull-dogged man, now sheriff, was in the van.

Behind him were Nathan Hayes and a half dozen others—two grinning Spear punchers, four others who were strangers to Johnny. Vardaman pushed up alongside Johnny. He had a pair of handcuffs in his hand. He lifted them—then paused.

"You make a move, Raff, and you'll walk downstairs into Hell!" he said with slow deadliness. "Cover him, boys!"

"It wouldn't hurt my feelings a bit," Nathan Hayes said humorously, "to *have* him try to break down the timber."

Johnny submitted to the handcuffing. One of the strangers swung down at Vardaman's order, to take Johnny's own saddle rope and cut it into lengths convenient for coupling his ankles together under his horse's belly. Vardaman unbuckled Johnny's shell belt and pulled the carbine from his scabbard. He secured the handcuff chain to the saddlefork with another piece of lariat. Then only did he look at Fierro.

"Another murder charge against you," he said grimly. "Well, Hayes, I certainly do thank you for the Spear's help in roping him. Thank the young lady for me, too. Tell her I'm mightily sorry her *vaquero* got downed in the roping, but them that's rubbed out is gone in a good cause."

Johnny stared from face to face. Then red rage got him. He had a gifted tongue. He used it, now, to sketch the family trees of Vardaman and Nathan Hayes. The sheriff sat stolidly under the lash of it, but as when Johnny had cursed him on the 77, Hayes's dark face went pale. He spurred furiously forward and struck at Johnny's face.

Johnny rolled his head away and dug the rowels into his horse. He cannoned into Hayes's mount, and Johnny's hard, bare head went like a battering ram into Hayes's face, Johnny lifting in the stirrups to add momentum. He smashed the Spear foreman back over the cantle, then leaned far out, trying to set his teeth in Hayes's throat. Someone rapped him with a pistol barrel, then caught his shoulder.

"We'll be leaving," Vardaman grunted. He rode up to get between Johnny and Hayes, who was spitting blood and teeth and swaying drunkenly in the saddle. "Come on, boys!"

The four strangers formed around Johnny. They left the two Spear punchers with Hayes, who seemed dazed beyond action. They took a stock trail leading north. All afternoon, they rode by dim trails or across open range. Johnny nodded to himself. Aden. The circuit court met there.

They made camp at dusk, and all night a watch was kept. Close watch, too. Every few minutes, the man on guard inspected Johnny's cuffs and rope lashings. As for Johnny, he got no sleep at all. He could not, for he knew Vardaman fairly well, and he had been looking at the sheriff when Vardaman had sent that word of thanks to Elenore Lovess. If Nathan Hayes had said that Elenore had helped trap him, he would have laughed and thought nothing of it. But Vardaman had no gift for lying. His face had been perfectly calm, natural, when he said, "Thank the young lady for me."

"And then, there was Fierro, too," Johnny must remind himself. "Fierro never took orders from anybody but Elenore or Hugh Lovess, and few from Hugh. He was Elenore's man, her private property. But I don't any more *believe* that she would do it . . ."

He ate breakfast in a grim silence that matched Vardaman's and that of two possemen. The other two deputies, with side glances at him, discussed the details of many hangings. Johnny turned scornfully to them after a while, "If you two slop barrel faces are yapping for my benefit, you might as well save your breath. You'll need it for bumming drinks off drunk Mexicans."

"Yeah?" cried one of them, jumping up angrily. "You down a few men from behind and you think you . . ."

Johnny drew up his bound feet and pushed them swiftly up into the deputy's belly. The man staggered backward, sat down in the cooking fire, and scrambled out ablaze, yelling and slapping himself. The others applauded him enthusiastically. Only Vardaman's stolid face was unchanged. He got up and spoke with authority.

"Come on! Cut it out! I don't want no more of this foolishness. I'm going to lodge him in Aden jail by noon."

The last ten miles into Aden was a sort of triumphal processional for Vardaman and the swaggering possemen. Mexicans and Anglos pressed up to stare at Johnny. Some of the talk was hostile, but by no means all. Among the Mexicans, and particularly among the Mexican women and girls, there was sympathy. "*Jovenito*"—"little young man"—they called him, and "*pobrecito*"—"poor little one." They shook black heads sorrowfully and hoped that he would win free.

Aden . . . He found himself riding through the passageway down which the four of them had run that night of the release, and there was the same fat turnkey whom he had held up then. Johnny grinned at him. "Hi, *hombre*! I'm back for a visit with you. I would have brought the little pistol, but I gave it to a goat herder. He was ashamed to take it, but he did for friendship and said he would let his child have it for a toy, to frighten Aden jailers with. I hope that the hotel is comfortable now?"

"More comfortable than . . ." the turnkey grinned and made the motion and the gesture of a man strangling.

Johnny laughed. They cut the rope from his ankles, and he swung stiffly down. He followed the turnkey, with Vardaman and the possemen crowding at his heels, into the cell tier. A door clanged behind him and Vardaman. The sheriff unlocked the handcuffs and went outside. The turnkey locked the cell door.

This was the old Spanish jail with cells of hewn stone blocks. There was a window, no more than ten inches square, giving light from the patio. It was barred. By dragging over a bench under it, Johnny could look out.

In mid-afternoon, he saw Zeke Martinez coming through the patio with a tall, lean Mexican who wore a badge and two pistols. The turnkey came out of his cubicle and joined them. Johnny sat down and waited. Presently, there was the clang of the door opening. In the dim light, he saw Martinez standing at the door of his cell. Martinez's grin was catlike.

"You're going to try cheating the Devil once too often, Zeke," Johnny said cheerfully. "I would have sworn that I got you in the office. Well! Better luck next time."

"My boy, there will be no next time—for you."

"When do I go to trial?" Johnny inquired.

"The day after tomorrow. You will first be tried for the murder of Annear. Kesall will be the witness. I think that a first-degree conviction will not be so hard to get, but in case you are not sentenced to hang, we will try you next for murdering Manuel Chavez. I have many witnesses for that."

"But you'd rather not try me on the Chavez charge, if you can help it," Johnny nodded with perfect understanding. "Because you don't want the Friarson mortgages you stole mentioned in court. You're not half so slick as you think, Zeke Martinez. Some of us see through you without much trouble."

Martinez laughed quite naturally and turned away. The turnkey brought beans and *tortillas* and coffee at dusk. Johnny asked him about Lieutenant Serrells.

"Surely, I know him," the turnkey nodded. "He is of the Governor's staff. He is now at Mesita with the Governor."

"At Mesita? And why is the Governor at Mesita?"

"He investigates conditions for himself, concerning the war that is threatened between the two sides."

That night and the next day dragged interminably for Johnny. The possemen had robbed him of everything he had—his money, even his tobacco and papers and matches. In mid-afternoon, when the turnkey came in for the second time, Johnny got a corn-husk cigarette from him. But the turnkey hung about the door, this time. Johnny watched him curiously. The fat man was a perfect statue of perplexity.

"*Juancito*," he said at last, "I am in the very devil of a fix. I am a poor man with many children. And I make but little here. So, when a lovely lady offers me money, it is hard to say 'no' to her."

Johnny leaned his shoulder on the door and looked curiously through at the moon-faced one. That all of this concerned him, he was sure. But how? "A lovely lady—" What lovely lady of Aden would be interested in him?

"But I have made up my mind! I will do it! I have nothing against you, *Juancito*! I would be glad to see you ride free, out of Aden. So I will take this lady's money. Listen carefully, Juancito! At nine, tonight, I will come to the door here, most quietly. I will give you a pistol. I will unlock the door, and you will lock me in the cell. Then you will go and take the horse that will be tied at the hitch rack in the street. Tomorrow . . . well! Six men held me up and locked me in the cell from which they freed you! I will do it, yes."

"Who is this lovely lady?" Johnny demanded scowling.

"She said that you would ask," the turnkey grinned, nodding wisely, "but you are not to know until—well, you will learn in her good time. Now, I must go. I have things to do. That horse to get and place at the hitch rack. *Amor de Dios*! I hope that they believe my tale tomorrow morning. Else Martinez will have my head!"

He waddled out, muttering to himself, and he did not appear at dusk. Johnny was the only prisoner at the moment. Evidently, the turnkey thought that supper was an unimportant item to a man about to escape trial for murder. Johnny gave the meal no thought. He was puzzling that phrase "a lovely lady." Could it be, could it possibly be, Elenore Lovess? He shook his head bewilderedly. If not Elenore—then whom? If Elenore—why?

"I don't believe she had a thing to do with that bushwhacking," he told himself, "but if she did, she might have got a change of heart . . . and I'll know all 'in her good time.' Well! I reckon I have got her to thank, whoever she is!"

Outside, the darkness grew thicker. It seemed many hours since he had heard the bells sounding the Angelus. Across the patio showed for a time a lean rectangle of golden light, where the door of the turnkey's cubicle was half-open, then it vanished. There was left to Johnny only the intermittent padding of feet on the street outside the passage.

Softly, the door of the cell tier opened. Johnny walked to the cell door. He could hear the labored breathing of the turnkey, louder than the scuff of the heavy feet.

CHAPTER 23

"*Juancito*!" came the rasping whisper. "*Cuerpo de Dios*! This is no business for a fat man—a man of family!"

The key clanked noisily against the lock plate. Johnny grinned. The fellow's hand was shaking. But the key found the keyhole at last and the door squeaked open. Johnny stepped out into the narrow corridor. The turnkey pressed a pistol against his hand. Johnny took it.

"Now! You tie me with rope! You put this handkerchief over my mouth and lock me inside. *Amor de Dios*! If tomorrow they do not believe me, I will be locked here in real truth. Martinez is set upon your hanging!"

Swiftly, Johnny tied fat wrists together and made a gag of the handkerchief. Then he locked the cell door and went silently down the corridor and around the elbow to stand for a moment listening at the jail door. What guards would there be? Surely, if Zeke Martinez were so set upon his hanging, there would be more guards than usual—to prevent such a jail delivery as he had worked for Ralph Naile and Dick Quell.

He looked down into the black darkness as if to see the pistol. He wondered how many shots he had—five, or six? He worked the ejector. The plunger entered a chamber, but no cartridge fell into his cupped palm. Incredulously, he spun the cylinder a trifle and again pushed the ejector. That chamber, too, was empty. Johnny's mouth tightened. Chamber by chamber, he investigated. Then he turned grimly back to the cell. He unlocked the door.

In the waistband of the turnkey's trousers, in back, he found a stubby .45 single action. The barrel had been sawed off back to the ejector end. The pistol was loaded in six chambers.

"Up!" he whispered fiercely. "Up, you dog! And come with me. Up, I tell you! Else I will certainly kill you here!"

Mumbling noises came from the gagged mouth. The turnkey was quivering like a great jelly. Savagely, Johnny prodded him out and down the corridor. At the door, they stopped. Johnny fumbled with the heavy iron latch. Almost soundlessly, he lifted it. He drew a deep breath, then with almost the same motion, he shoved the door wide open with a foot and sent the turnkey staggering out into the patio.

There was a fusillade, flames darting from a half dozen weapons posted on the sides of the door. The men ran at the sprawling figure ten feet out from the doorway. They were a dark mass over the fallen man. At point-blank range, they fired into him . . . Johnny heard their grunts and snarlings.

He edged out behind them and flattened himself against the wall. The turnkey's pistol was trained on the group. Step by step, he moved away from where they were now standing over the body. Three steps; four; five . . . He was ten or twelve feet up the wall toward the passage mouth. Men came running through it, running across the patio. They were yelling excitedly. Yelling questions—that proved their knowledge of this plan.

Johnny kept edging along the wall. The feet thudded by, carrying the dark figures past him. He made the corner. Then a fierce cry from the body told of the discovery of the mistake.

"Quick!" Zeke Martinez roared. "Into the jail, some of you fools! This is not the man. He must still be inside! Unless . . ."

Johnny worked up the wall. He made the passage mouth. Men came running that way, apparently to block the passage's end. He ran noiselessly toward the street. There was no horse at the hitchrack. He ran across the street and turned toward the center of Aden. And a dark column came riding up the street toward him. He went over a high wall and dropped into a garden. This, he knew, was the Governor's Palace.

A gate opened, and horses came tramping up the driveway. Johnny moved over to the shelter of a shrub and looked out. Lights came out of the house. He saw Governor Yager swing down from a horse and go stiffly past a lighted window to disappear. Presently, the horses were all in the stable, and the sounds had died away. Johnny lay and watched that window.

The horses in the stable would be weary from their day. But there might be some fresh ones there. Past the window, he saw the Governor go. He moved until he could look into the room. Yager sat down and stretched lazily. Then he straightened, sitting at a long table. He began to shuffle some papers. Johnny moved back and forth until he could see every corner of the far side of the room. Nobody was there.

Then a door opened. Lieutenant Serrells burst in. He was excited. He talked with jerky little movements of hand and head. Yager listened stiffly, then slowly shook his head. He shrugged and looked at his papers again. Serrells turned and went out, closing the door behind him. Yager got up from the table and came to the window. He looked out, as if trying to stare over the wall at the street, from which came now yells and the thud of hoofs.

He shook his gray head and went back to the table. But instead of picking up his papers again, he sat staring at the far wall, blankly. Johnny wriggled across to the window. It was a casement, opening in. It was latched. He rapped lightly upon a pane. Yager turned, frowning. Johnny rapped again. Yager got up and came to look through it.

"Who is it?" he asked but opened the window without waiting for an answer. Johnny went up like a cat and squatted on the sill, grinning at the Governor, who had stepped back.

"Sorry I have to break in on you like this, Governor," he said grimly. "I never intended to. I sent you word by the little soldier that I didn't dare put my head into this rattlers' den, but some Mesita people decided that I'd better come to Aden. So here I am. And if you still want to talk to me . . ."

He stepped off the sill to the floor, standing a little away from the casement. Yager, staring at him steadily, shook his head. His face was hard and unfriendly.

"I don't think I do, now. When I sent you that message, that invitation, I didn't know all that I've learned since. I was following your advice, which seemed good advice, to investigate conditions at first hand. I thought that you might very well be the man to give me a great deal of what we might call the other side of affairs—the side that you indicated is opposed to the side I'd heard."

Johnny nodded and began to whistle almost soundlessly, meeting the Governor's eyes levelly. "And you have got this other side's story, now. You heard them testify, same as if you were holding court. You balanced one against the other, and at the last, you had to decide that I'm guilty of everything they charge against me, and that Zeke Martinez is the snow-white ram lamb."

For a moment, the Governor looked vaguely uncomfortable. He moved his shoulders irritably.

"I went to Mesita. I talked to representative citizens of that vicinity. And—not one of them had a good word to say for you or your gang, Raff!"

Johnny shrugged, looking down at the sawed-off Colt in his hand. He moved slightly. "Then I reckon *this* is my only dependence," he said. "If you talked to the representative men in and around Mesita, and not one of 'em said that I'd ever done a good deed, or could be expected to, there's no use taking your time. I'll be leaving you the way I came in. You have to give the alarm, of course, as soon as I stop threatening you with this pistol. But that's all right. Nobody will take me alive again.

"So—" Slowly, he grinned at Yager. There was amusement, a shade of mockery in the grin.

"*Adiós*, Your Excellency. I'll bet that, back in New Britain, you're a good fellow to know, and I have got no right to talk. Chances are, if I went to Connecticut and settled down to live there, I'd be as easy to hornswoggle as a Connecticut man is in this country. I'll say this for you folks: The two of you I've known, I've liked. Ed Friarson was the best friend I ever had. The only thing against him was that he couldn't hold his own at skullduggery, and he leaned backward so far, trying to wait for the law to protect his rights, that he fell over and got killed." He was turning to the window when Yager's sharp word stopped him. He looked back at the Governor.

"Not so fast! I won't have you go, feeling that I haven't been fair with you. I have! And I'm not going to be put in the wrong. You mentioned Friarson. Well, from what I've heard of him, he was a troublemaker. He practiced usury, bought stolen stock, encouraged murder, and committed murder himself. I heard nothing from anybody, of any such side of him as this you're describing. As for you, Raff, Mesita seems to agree that you're a multiple murderer, a stock thief, a highway robber—and I don't know what else! At the time I sent Lieutenant Serrells to you, it seemed to me possible that you were a young man who hadn't got precisely a fair deal; that you might have been pushed by an older, shrewder man, Friarson, into criminal ways. It seemed to me that you might tell me a great deal about the High Mesa country, from a cowboy's viewpoint, and, too, be given a chance to get out of outlawry. When Lieutenant Serrells came back, his report was that you were nothing but a drunken killer. And now he tells me that you've just murdered the turnkey and escaped jail!"

"Then—why are you calling me back?" Johnny demanded in a puzzled voice. "You thought that, but now you know better—I've been the tool of an older man—Excuse me if that seems funny! Ed Friarson was a hell of a fine fellow, but if he had lived to be a thousand, he never would have known the half of what I've learned about people we have to deal with in this country. As for pushing me into outlawry, about the last thing that Ed said to me was that he worried about his partner in Mesita doing something illegal. That was why we headed for town that day last month."

He stared frowningly at the frowning Governor. "Did Hugh Lovess and Gibb Mollison and Orville Atchley and Walt Jefferies and Judge Kent Biddle and Lewis Talbot tell you that I was a murdering thief and holdup man," he asked slowly, "or did you talk to 'em at all?"

Very sardonically, he grinned. "In other words, you hardly know who they are! I thought so. You see, when you went down to Mesita, you had a little list of 'representative citizens' to see. Zeke Martinez gave it to you, and he sent word ahead so that they'd meet you: Zagin and Whitey Kew and Joe Downer and Jink Kesall—why, what's the matter, Governor?"

He laughed shortly. "You talked to Ring men, and they told the tale scary, and you listened, and you said 'oh, dear!' and maybe 'my God!' and you came home. Yes, sir! You came home from a trip you might as well not have made, for it was nothing but a Martinez tour and you didn't find out a thing you didn't already know."

He turned back to the window. This time, he listened for sounds outside that would tell of searchers in the palace garden. He could hear nothing but distant calls on the street that indicated—he thought—a house-to-house hunt for him.

"Wait a minute, Raff," Yager called to him. There was a shade of uncertainty in the Governor's voice. "I try to be fair, and some things you've said—perhaps the way you said them, as much as anything—make me wonder. Suppose you tell me your story—sit down here. You can hardly lose anything. I can't compound a felony by letting you go. But on the other hand, if you were to shut that window and bar the door, I couldn't keep you here if you decided to leave. So . . ."

Johnny faced him again. He nodded.

"All right! It's a fairly long tale. But it's about time you heard it! The whole story of what happened in the Mesita country, up on the Rio Vaca, and in Mesita. And what's been going on right here in Aden, up to the time less than an hour ago, when that turnkey handed me an empty pistol and told me that he'd been bribed to let me break jail—and I pushed him through the door ahead of me, and Zeke Martinez's gang killed him for me."

He closed the window and turned the catch, then pulled a curtain across it. He went over to the door and dropped the thick bar in its sockets. Yager had crossed the room to a cupboard. He brought out a squat, black bottle, two glasses, a box of cigars. He put them on a table and motioned toward a chair.

Johnny took a cigar and lit it. The Governor poured brandy from the black bottle into their glasses and lifted his own. Johnny's sandy brows climbed.

"You'll drink with an outlaw?" he said grimly.

"There are outlaws and outlaws," Yager shrugged cheerfully, "but at the present moment you're merely a Source of Information. As such, you're entitled to such small pleasures as I can give you, if eighteen-year-old Brissac can be termed a small pleasure."

"Thanks! I came into this country riding the chuckline with another Texas man named Wright—'Noisy' Wright. A good puncher, but a damn poor man. We worked all around. For Veck and Zagin at Mesita, first. We quit them after six months or so. They offered us five hundred to lie up behind Gibb Mollison's Flying M house and kill him. I wouldn't, and Noisy was afraid to, and Gibb Mollison is alive today, because they got the yellow up in their necks for fear I'd tell about the offer if they got somebody else to kill him."

He drank his brandy and put the glass down.

"We went over to the Spear, and I busted horses for Hugh Lovess while Noisy rode on the little drives that the Spear's always making. I'm a better rider than Noisy, else I would have mixed more than I did, in handling the wet stock that every big outfit in this country buys and sells. I worked for the Spear for over a year. Then—well, there was a row. Nothing to do with my work. It was—personal. Lovess fired me."

"I heard about that," the Governor nodded. His mouth jerked at a corner. "You lifted your eyes too high and someone, not the young crown princess, told Lovess."

"Anyway," Johnny shrugged uncomfortably, "Veck and Zagin wanted me to come back to 'em. I wouldn't, because I knew what it would lead to. They're Martinez's partners down there, and whether you want to believe it or not, Martinez just about bosses the High Mesa country, now, and he intends to own it before he's done. He's a thief and a killer and a damn brave man, but I wouldn't work for him. Then—Edward Friarson came down here for his lungs. He had money. He had brains, too—of a particular kind. He hired me to help him start a horse ranch up on the Vaca. He . . ."

The Governor lifted his brows inquiringly as Johnny laughed. "What's the joke?" he asked and poured them more Brissac.

"He hired me because he'd been inquiring

around and he liked what he'd heard about my handling of horses. But the chief reason he hired me was that I'd never shot at a man! Friarson deplored killings. I learnt the word from listening to him do it, day in and day out, all the year and more that I was with him. Friarson was like an older brother to me, in lots of ways . . ."

CHAPTER 24

"It's simply incredible!" the Governor said slowly, two hours later, when the tale was ended, covering the time from Friarson's arrival in Mesita to the shots that killed the turnkey.

He shook his head and reached for the Brissac bottle. Johnny put down the stub of his third cigar and looked uncertainly at Yager. "It's just natural!" he shrugged. "Just what the likes of Martinez and Veck and Zagin and the others would do, any time they could, and this was the time they could do it."

"I know that," Yager nodded. "But still, it's incredible that they could have done all the things they have done. I'd find it hard to believe your story, Raff, except for one thing: Even those men of Mesita, who can't find words hard enough to describe you, date your history from Friarson's death on the Rio Vaca road. Before then, you seem not to have signified to anybody. You were just a—what do you call it—top hand cowboy and the best rider in all the country. But still, just a drifting cowboy of no importance."

Johnny nodded and watched Yager fumble absently with the accumulation of mail upon the table. The Governor looked up at him abruptly and nodded, like a man arrived at a decision.

"I have unlimited authority. I'm not bound by statute or anything else. I can settle these troubles as I see fit. So—if you'll give me your word to leave here, go to Texas—go anywhere beyond my jurisdiction, I'll formally clear you of everything charged against you. I'm doing this on the strength of my judgment of you. If I'm mistaken, then I'm a hundred percent mistaken. Will you accept my offer? You see that you can't stay in the High Mesa country. Too many hate you; you hate too many. Within a month, you'd be in trouble again. So you have to go, and I'll try to clean up conditions in every direction. Remove these shooting officers and weak judges."

Johnny shook his head, staring at the drink in his hand. "I can't. I—I certainly wish I could," he said in a low voice. Then he straightened, emptied his glass, and stood up with shoulders squared. "No, I can't do it. If I leave inside six months, everything will be about the way it has been. Martinez and Zagin will be running things. An honest man will be robbed blind, unless he's quick on the shoot, and if he's that way, some hired bushwhacker will knock him over. You might keep 'em straight for a while. But you're not going to be here forever. Governors come and go. You're the second I've seen in less than three years. You'll go and then . . ."

He snapped his fingers. "Martinez will pull the wool over the new Governor's eyes. He's plenty slick. You're no fool, but he hoodwinked you. No! I'll just have to take my chances and go on until I'm stopped with a chunk of lead or a rope or something. I'm sick of the whole damned business. I wish I could walk out of here and hang up my guns and never take 'em down again, but the way it looks to me, I'm the only man to straighten out the mess, and my way is the only way to straighten it."

There was a lengthy silence. Yager pushed the letters around on the table, then he frowned as one seemed to catch his eye. He picked it up, tore open the envelope. Johnny waited with growing impatience and glances at the window through which he would disappear. But Yager skimmed the several sheets of the letter rapidly and seemed to have forgotten him.

"Well," Johnny broke in upon him politely, "I reckon I'll be going. And I thank you for hearing me out—and for the entertainment—"

"Sit down! Sit down!" Yager said impatiently. "Let me think. Let—me—think . . ."

He frowned blankly at the far wall for a moment, then:

"What was it you asked me about Friarson, that day in Dolores's place? Well, I told you that I didn't know him; that he was a Hartford man. Odd! I told you truthfully that I'd heard his name and no more. But you didn't mention Edward Friarson's sister, so I didn't know that

Mrs. Gail of Hartford is, or was, his sister, and I do know her, intimately. This," he held up the letter, "is from her. It's about the Mesita trouble. She encloses letters of Friarson's, antedating the murder! Letters that vividly describe conditions as you described them. He seems to have been very fond of you and to have trusted you completely. Also, she sends a letter written to her by Judge Kent Biddle, and I seem to have misjudged Biddle."

Johnny sat down again, more than a little bewildered, and the Governor picked up the several sections of Mrs. Gail's letter and re-read them. Time passed. Yager put down the pages, at last, and stared at the ceiling. Slowly, his chin came down, and he looked at Johnny intently, as if analyzing him feature by feature. His mouth was grim, his eyes bright.

"Biddle's letter to Mrs. Gail remarks that the judge holds the conviction that, of all the men in the High Mesa country, there is only one qualified in every respect to act as sheriff at Mesita. And he says, 'With Zeke Martinez at the Governor's ear, telling him what to see, what to hear, what to believe, and what to do, of course, young Raff will never be Sheriff of Mesita . . .' "

"There's nothing wrong with Kent Biddle's head," Johnny nodded dryly, "even if I was a candidate."

"Vardaman is still in town," the Governor

said thoughtfully. "I am going to talk to him. Desperate cases require desperate remedies, so I'll do the desperate thing: I'm going to call Vardaman in tomorrow morning. I'm going to show him my proclamation about you. I'm going to demand of him, under penalty of his removal from office, that he—"

He stopped, staring up smilingly at the ceiling, as if upon that white plaster he pictured a scene that pleased him. He nodded. "I'm going to tell him to make you chief deputy!"

"Huh?" Johnny cried, gaping. "Chief deputy? You'd make the prize criminal of the country chief deputy?"

"Ah . . . But," the Governor looked across at him, almost purred, "you'll be as white as the chosen lamb, chemically pure, legally irreproachable, when my proclamation is published. Vardaman has just been the beneficiary of a special election that they steamrolled through, up there. He's now sheriff. I'm going to demand that you be chief deputy. Also, I'm going to whisper in Vardaman's ear that he is to make no move without your approval. *You* are sheriff of Mesita County and more! You are my personal representative. The High Mesa country understands force, does it? By God! I'll give it to them! I'm putting faith in you."

"You won't be sorry. I will swear that on a stack of Bibles!" Johnny said grimly. "But,

Governor, Zagin and that crowd up there, they're not going to like this, you know. In fact, they wouldn't like it if it had sugar on it! They will work on Vardaman. Do one thing more, to make what you are doing now mean something: In that proclamation you're going to write, put in the names of Ralph Naile, Richard Quell, and High Pockets Sill—his real name is Regulus—and make Vardaman appoint 'em deputies. Then I'll have a force to work with."

"All right! Now, you catch some sleep on that couch."

CHAPTER 25

Noon. Johnny Raff, coming boldly up the street to turn in at the palace entrance, stopped for an instant to stare up and down and shake his head.

"I feel like the old lady in the Mother Goose rhyme," he muttered to himself. " 'Can this be really I?' Chief deputy, actually sheriff of Mesita County . . . I wonder how Nathan Hayes is going to like that . . . no—I know how he'll like it!"

He looked down at himself. From hat to boots, he was a new man, bathed and shaved and wearing a brand-new outfit. Only gun, holster, and belt were old—his own, recovered with horse and saddle from Vardaman. Longest, he looked at the star which Vardaman had taken from one of the possemen to give him. He went in.

"Have you chanced to see any special excitement on the street?" the Governor inquired, smilingly. "Zeke Martinez went before the Grand Jury this morning. He now lies under indictment for forgery. You see, Johnny Raff, I employed a young man named Cristoforo Palacios for a while. But Cristoforo was entirely too clever with his pen. We had to part with him, and he was immediately hired by Martinez, at approximately the time that forged transfer of mortgages must have been done. I interviewed Cristoforo this morning, and I had before me the transfer—we knew where Judge Biddle kept his papers here and got it. Cristoforo, with just a trifle of pressure, admitted the forgery and confessed that he had been paid twenty dollars by Martinez. So . . ."

"Better pick the jury mighty careful," Johnny said cynically. "But, either way, it's a step in the right direction. Now . . . Vardaman's ready to go, and so am I."

He shook hands with the Governor and with the stiff, disapproving young Lieutenant Serrells. Back to the street, then, to the corral where Vardaman waited. The possemen were no longer deputies. Vardaman had discharged them. His red face was sullen. But even so slow-witted a man could see the truth of what Governor Yager had pointed out: Even though he was to exercise no power as sheriff, the fees and emoluments of the office yet were his. So he looked now at Johnny.

"I'll save you some trouble, as soon as we hit Mesita," Johnny grinned. "I'll do some talking to Zagin. When I'm done, I don't think he'll bear down heavy on you, Vardaman."

There was a quiet little hotel on the right side of the street that they must pass going out. Johnny, chancing to look sidelong, could have sworn that a woman peered out of a doorway, staring at them. But when he looked more closely, she was gone. He shook his head, frowning slightly. "Now . . . why should that remind me of what that lying turnkey said? 'A beautiful lady—' But he must've been lying about everything. There was no beautiful lady mixed into *that* deal."

They were ten miles down the southern road when a dust cloud ahead was translated into three fast-riding men. Johnny stared, then grinned at Vardaman.

"There come our other three proclamation Ikes. Ralph Naile, Dick Quell, and Regulus High Pockets Sill. Our three new deputies. You can swear 'em in right here. I'll tell 'em what has happened. Then you can swear 'em in without being bitten before they come to. Let me handle the business."

The three recognized Johnny at a distance. This was proved by the wild yell of Ralph Naile and the added speed of the rabbit-jumping horses. They pulled in before Johnny and Vardaman. But Johnny, nose in air, waved them off.

"Kindly stay off to the side," he invited them. "I'm a changed man. I'm living a higher, nobler life now. I can't associate with common outlaws anymore. Me, *I'm* a chief deputy."

Ralph Naile, finding the bead pointed star on Johnny's shirt, yelled wildly once more. He lifted Johnny bodily from the saddle and balanced him on a huge palm overhead.

"Say you're lying or I'll drop you into the

dirt and mess your fine, new breeches!" he threatened.

"Let me down, and I'll tell you," Johnny grinned. "Easy! With proper respect for the weight and majesty of the Law. You three are deputies of Mesita County. Yeah . . . Vardaman, here, has had a plumb complete total change of heart. He was aiming to see me hang two days back. Now . . ."

"Now," Vardaman admitted with a grim sort of humor, "this crazy hairpin is sheriff of Mesita. But I have got the pocketbook. So far as badge flapping is concerned, he and you others can do it. I'll collect the money and keep it!"

Swiftly, he swore in the three and then rode on, leaving the four of them to follow, Johnny telling his incredible story, the others grunting, swearing, shaking heads in amazement. At the end, Ralph told their part. "We went hunting you—you *omadhaun*! And we found where the dirty deed was done. But we lost the trail a time or two. We were coming to take up Aden jail by the roots and wave her around our heads and fling her across the line and let her squash . . ."

"Gracious!" Johnny cried. "With me in it, all the time. Think of that, Ralph, maybe I'd have got squashed too. Dick, did you find out anything at the Flying M?"

"Mollison says something is wrong between Lovess and Nathan Hayes," Dick shrugged. "One of Mollison's riders was holed up on the Spear range, kind of looking around. Lovess and Hayes and some Spear waddies rode along the arroyo he had just topped out of. Rode right under him. They were fussing like cats on a clothes line, he says. Lovess says something to Hayes about getting along without him for some years, and maybe he can do the same now, if he needs to. He says Hayes maybe has made a little mistake; Hugh Lovess owns the Spear, not Hayes . . ."

"Well!" Johnny cried. "When the thieves fall out—"

He was very thoughtful, from then until the moment that the party rode up to the 77 house, near dusk, and got down to stay for the night. Walt Jefferies merely grunted at the sight of the transformed party, for word had gone from Aden of the Governor's amazing action. Johnny wondered how far, in what particular directions, that word had carried. To the Spear? He hoped so.

After supper, Johnny drew Jefferies outside. When they leaned against the corral bars in the moonlight, he looked steadily at the 77 owner.

"What'd Hayes want, Walt," he asked quietly, "today?"

"Hayes? Why—Why, Johnny, what makes you say Hayes?"

"Walt, your honesty is a new-made thing, of course," Johnny said, "and it ought to be all the more precious and all that. Now, if you keep on stuttering, you'll bear out my suspicions of you. I saw Hayes's horse tracks at your door. I know those horseshoes! Now, I like to have things out in the daylight. I'm funny that way. Wait a minute, though! Let me tell you a thing or two. Maybe it'll make talking come slicker to you:

"The Governor handed Vardaman plenty of orders, and Vardaman will damn certain abide by 'em, but Vardaman hasn't been told the half! I'm not only the real sheriff of Mesita, I'm the personal representative of the Governor! Did you know that Zeke Martinez is going to the pen for forgery? Walt, that's the beginning of the smash! This is going to be the year the prairie burns! Governor Yager has unlimited authority to clean up this mess we're all tired of hearing about, and I have got the whole United States Government behind me, if I need it. All right! I am going to make this a place where you can leave your door unbarred at night, where you can go off and leave a cow on the range and come back and find it! Now—Well, Walt, now that you have figured, is there something, some little, tiny thing, that you'd like to tell a fellow? Just anything!"

"He has had a squabble with Lovess, about something," Walt Jefferies said sulkily, "I don't know what. But he's black mad, Johnny. I wouldn't want to cross him. He's got that little grin on his mouth, and his eyes look kind of red.

I saw him like that, once before. He rode into Bravo that time, and he just brazenly shot three tinhorns full of holes in Quinn Evans's Crystal for cheating him and letting the word get out. He's got something up his sleeve, Johnny. He hinted around and wanted to know if I would like to be on his side and make something."

"Didn't he say a thing that would give you a notion? I knew he'd rowed with Lovess, and there's no use in your bothering about what the trouble was. You'll find out soon enough," Johnny said airily, as if he knew all about it.

"No. He wasn't ready to talk right out, looked like, but he wanted me and the two boys with him, he says. He'll be back in a day or two to get my final word and show his cards. How'd you know he'd been here and rowed with Lovess?"

"Walt," Johnny said solemnly, "I'll bet you couldn't put on a pair of new boots, but I'd hear 'em squeak inside two days, even if I was in jail in Aden. It's all in having folks scattered around that are willing to tell things. Friends of mine that nobody'd take for friends of mine. So be honest, Walt."

It was a badly worried Jefferies whom they left the next morning. Johnny grinned. That artistic touch about informants everywhere would rankle and, if compulsion didn't prove too strong in the other direction, might keep Walt Jefferies honest.

Zagin stood in the doorway of the store as the quintet rode into town. His hands were folded upon his stomach. His hollow blue eye was squinted against the up-wreathing smoke of the inevitable fat Habana. Ken Vardaman watched him for fifty yards. Zagin was a benevolent, paternal figure, but the sheriff seemed to take no pleasure from watching him. Johnny pushed up a little, and Vardaman let him lead.

"Ah, Johnny!" Zagin nodded, "This is fine, no? All the troubles gone. *Ja*! Vardaman will be sheriff in the name; Johnny Raff will be sheriff in the fact. Fine, Johnny!"

"Where's my old friend, Jink Kesall?" Johnny grinned. "You know, Zagin, I kind of looked for Kesall to make a—well, a welcoming committee. In fact, I have been looking for him for the last ten miles. He around?"

"Jink has the madness. He sulks because *he* was not the sheriff elected. I have talked, but . . ." he shrugged placidly. "Jink, he have resign. He will punch cows again."

Johnny swung down. He grunted to the others to go on. He motioned Zagin inside the store, and they went elbow to elbow, back to the office. Johnny took a cigar and looked about him. There were a few customers, but none stood within earshot.

"Different, now, Zagin," he said slowly. "You offered me the star, once, and—damn your black, shiny old soul—I believe you meant it. I wouldn't take it because . . ."

"Because you was the honest young fool," Zagin nodded. "You would not take it and take the order from us. And now?"

"Now, I've got it, but instead of you telling me what to do, I'll tell you, and, Zagin, you had better listen!"

"Who? Me? Johnny, I likes you! Sure, I listen!"

"Things are going to be different—mightily different, and you had better change with the times. You've got sense enough to know that you don't swim a dry arroyo. So, if you rest contented with the money you've got and the place you've got, now that Veck's out of the way, you and this sheriff's office will get along fine."

"Sure! We always gets along, Johnny! And now . . ."

There was the sound of shots, from some little distance. Muffled shots. Johnny raced to the door of the store. He looked down the street, toward the adobe building that was Mesita's courthouse. There was nobody on that side of the street within forty yards. Men on the other side, popping out of saloons and stores, stared at the courthouse, and out of the building now came a man—Kenneth Vardaman.

He leaned wearily against the wall for an instant, then he moved as if to cross the street.

Suddenly, he collapsed to sprawl across the sidewalk. He lay very still.

Johnny ran with pistol out, toward him. He kept close to the walls of the buildings, so that nobody could shoot at him from door or window. With some difficulty, he got to Vardaman and looked sidelong at the office door, from which Vardaman had come. From inside, he heard the scrape of soft footsteps.

He slid quietly toward it and ventured to peep inside.

CHAPTER 26

There was nobody in the sheriff's office. But there was a door through which one could go from the office into the courtroom, and to the open air behind. Johnny ran inside on tiptoes. Nobody was in the courtroom. He ran across it. There was a back door, and he looked out, but no one was in sight. He followed the bootprints he saw, and as he trailed the killer of Vardaman, he speculated about the killer.

"Kesall's not in town, so Zagin said, and who, besides Jink, would feel like killing Vardaman? If Jink felt like it, and had nerve enough to buck Zagin . . ."

There was no present answer to that. He met a group of men. None had seen anyone coming that way. He looked over their shoulders and caught sight of Judge Biddle standing on the street, looking down at him between buildings.

"Glad to see you, Johnny Raff! Glad to see you indeed—this way," the little Judge smiled. "Have you any idea who killed Vardaman? For he's dead, very dead, without a word. No? Then, may I suggest Jink Kesall as a candidate?"

"Zagin told me Kesall's not in town," Johnny frowned.

"I have to correct that statement. Kesall not

only is in town, but he has been in town, if not apparent to everyone, since dawn. He has been at his girl's house. I happened to see him riding in, and sometimes it pays to have, and use, glasses."

"Nobody saw the killing," Johnny meditated. "So, if Kesall is in town and can manage to sit down nice and quiet somewhere, who's to say he's a killer? You have got to have evidence."

He moved up the street and then across, with Judge Biddle at his elbow. He looked in over the swinging doors of the Congress and did not find Kesall among the talking, gesticulating drinkers. But, on impulse, he pushed back the doors and went inside. Silence greeted him. As if by magic, the man the law had harried up and down the High Mesa country was now the law-bearer. They stared.

Johnny looked thoughtfully at each man in turn and spoke to none. He turned to look at the dusky rear of the place, and there was Jink Kesall, sitting in a tilted chair with back to wall, bootheels hooked in a round, hat down over the bridge of his hooked nose. His fierce face was darkly calm. Johnny could not tell by looking at him if he was asleep or awake.

Johnny moved toward him. Imperceptibly, almost, Kesall's neck stiffened, and his head moved backward. Two steps, and Johnny saw the glint of black eyes under the shadowing hat brim. Two more steps, and Kesall gave over all pretense. He pushed back his hat and sat with thumbs hooked in crossed shell belts.

"Did you kill Vardaman?" Johnny asked him, calmly. It did occur to him that here was, next only to Nathan Hayes, if second to Hayes, the most dangerous man in the country: the fastest on the draw, the most amazingly accurate on the shoot, but he looked down at Jink Kesall as if he were nobody.

"Vardaman?" Kesall repeated the name. "No, I haven't got a bean shooter—and it'd be a plumb shame to kill him with anything bigger. Ken was about your size as a gun-slinger."

"Where were you when the shooting happened, then?"

"None of your damn business, and if there's something else you want to know, take the same answer!"

"Oh, but I couldn't take an answer like that!" Johnny said softly. But as he stared down into the malignant dark eyes, a picture came to him of Edward Friarson, lying beside the road; of Kesall and Simon Jones, Heinie Eddieford and Tigre Lopez. The murder posse that Kesall had led.

He and Kesall were natural enemies. Johnny felt that if he had met this black, scowling cowboy in the middle of the desert, he would have hated him without pause for thought, but beyond that was the actual reason he had for hating him. He found his mouth suddenly dry, something like a red haze coming between him and Kesall, and a blazing fury that shook him. *Here!* he thought. *That would never do.* Not when Jink Kesall sat with hands all but on gun butts, before him.

He looked past Kesall's shoulder and mentally counted up to twenty. The haze vanished; his nerves steadied. "Come along, Kesall," he drawled. "We're going to match your bootprints with the tracks outside the back door of the courtroom. I have got a notion that maybe they'll fit!"

"We ain't going nowhere!" Kesall said grimly, "but you had better be going somewheres—damn fast! You come back with notions . . ."

"I said, come along!" Johnny almost whispered, "and, as a beginning, put your hands up and grab hold of your ears!"

Jink Kesall merely sat motionless. He was for all the world like a coiled snake, in the instant before striking. His dark eyes were unwaveringly upon Johnny's. Johnny very deliberately moved his gun hand. Kesall went into action with all the flashing speed he had the name for. His hands flipped to Colt butts. Thumbs dropped upon gun hammers. The stubby pistols twitched out. There was thick silence in the barroom.

But, as with Simon Jones here in this same barroom, Johnny had pushed the other man into action; knew that Kesall was going to draw before the man himself knew it; was ready for the move. The deliberation of his hand movement changed to a speed that more than matched Kesall's.

His gun was out, cocked, flaming, before Kesall's. Nor did he waste time or thought on so foolish a thing as trying to wing Kesall. He shot to kill. Nothing else would serve here with this killer. Kesall's chair came down upon all four legs. Right hand, left hand, he drove two bullets into the floor before he fell forward out of the chair.

Johnny turned, then, to face the men behind him, for Jink Kesall had owned some friends of his own hardcase sort. But if any were here now, if any thought about taking up Kesall's battle, discretion gripped them hard. Judge Biddle stood with a hand in each pocket, and Judge Biddle was known to carry a derringer in each of those pockets, wicked little .41s with which he was more than usually deadly. Besides, behind him, nearer the door, three tight-faced men stood, looking to right and left. Ralph Naile grinned suddenly and shoved a Mexican forward, "And that saves the county the price of some rope! For it was he who downed Vardaman. Here's a man that seen him run from the back door, putting away his pistol, Johnny."

Johnny nodded. Hugh Lovess had come into the Congress. He leaned on the bar, grim face interested, rather than hostile. When the small formalities of moving Kesall to a back room had been finished, Johnny shook off the men who wanted to talk about his speed and his luck. He moved up beside Lovess. "Hear you had some trouble with Hayes," he said when attention was no longer focused on him.

"What's it to you?" Lovess grunted. "A Spear row."

"Plenty. When he shoots you in the back, that'll be my affair. I'll have the job of catching him, you know."

"Hayes will do no shooting at me, and if you should take after him, Johnny, you better pray you can't catch him! That wasn't a thing compared to what Hayes can do."

"You know . . . I've got a notion," Johnny said thoughtfully. "My notion is, you're going to be yelling for help—my help, sooner than you want to admit. Elenore in town?"

"Home. But you're likely fooling yourself about my having to come to a kid cowboy for help, just because he happens to have a badge. Don't worry about affairs, Johnny."

Johnny stared at him, then shook his head. Something was on Hugh Lovess's mind. If it had not seemed foolish, Lovess being the man he was, Johnny would have said that he was worried, for he was being too courteous to be normal!

CHAPTER 27

Ralph Naile pushed his head inside the office door and spoke meditatively. It was a lovely and peaceful morning, the second to dawn upon Mesita since Vardaman's murder. It was the very loveliness and peace upon which Ralph remarked caustically, "I would not have been taking the damn badge," he said sourly, "had I known it was to mean living like a sheep herder. The damn county is asleep—not life enough to interest a cockroach."

He turned in the doorway at the distant sound of hoofbeats. He stared north, and Johnny, wrestling with the accumulated papers of the shrievalty, and with little head or enthusiasm for such work, watched him interestedly.

"It's Lovess," Ralph said. "It's—it's—" He was silent for so long that Johnny got up. "He's hurt!" Ralph grunted.

Johnny jumped to the door. Men were coming out of buildings, jumping off sidewalks; they were running out to the horse of Hugh Lovess, who swayed from side to side in the saddle. Lovess waved them off and continued toward the courthouse. Johnny sprinted after Ralph Naile.

"Johnny!" Lovess said thickly. "Johnny Raff! Go 'way, you all. Want Johnny Raff. I—got to—have help!"

His eyes were glazed. His face was ghastly white. The state of his clothing told that he must have fallen from the saddle and somehow got back again, more than once. He seemed literally caked with red mud. Johnny whirled upon the gapers. "Whiskey! And the doctor!" he yelled. "The man's dying."

He called Hugh Lovess. He put up his hands and eased the big body out of the saddle. Ralph Naile helped. They carried Lovess into a store. The doctor came on the run, a young medical student. He worked nervously fast. Hugh Lovess's eyes opened after a time:

"Johnny! It was Hayes. You were right. He shot me—last night. Left me for dead. Took the damn thieves he's been collecting on the Spear, and Whitey Kew and Joe Downer. They're stripping me—heading everything loose for the breaks, and for that rustlers' roost over at Hell Gate Arroyo. Figured I was dead—they'd be plumb gone before word got around. He'd scattered my honest boys from hell to breakfast."

Johnny yelled, "Where's Elenore? Was she there?"

Painfully, the eyes opened again. Lovess moved his lips stiffly. Johnny bent to him. Lovess stared—strained desperately to speak. "I don't know—where she is!" he whispered.

"Come on, you all!" Johnny snarled at Ralph and Dick and Sill. "I've got to throw a posse together. Hayes may have twenty men with him, counting the Heart and the D-Bar and his fancy thieves from the Spear bunkhouse. This was what he wanted Walt Jefferies and the 77 in on."

He separated his lieutenants swiftly and skillfully. They went to gather ammunition; to commandeer cooked food from houses and restaurants; to check on available horses. Johnny and Judge Biddle undertook to enlist the possemen.

It was slow work. But Johnny, chafing at the delay, had to admit that Biddle's recruiting was excellently done. If it had taken an hour, still it would mean greater speed in the time of fighting, to know that every man of the fourteen was one to depend upon, a fighter, an honest man, a stayer. They had good horses and good weapons. They had plenty of food and cartridges galore. Johnny lifted his hands in the air.

"Let's go!" he grunted. "Hell's bells! Let's go!"

He led them at the long, hard trot that meant six miles an hour and that all day long. He and Biddle and Lewis Talbot rode together, out on the road to the Spear. Ralph Naile and Dick Quell shortly spurred ahead. They would make the Flying M and the Flagg; pick up the riders of Mollison and Atchley. Johnny, brows scowlingly drawn against the June heat haze, spoke sidelong to Biddle and Talbot, "At a guess, from hearing what Lovess said, the herd may have a good long start. If Hayes told Lovess before he shot him all that he aimed to do, it sounds to me like the stripping had been done and the stuff was being shoved toward Hell Gate then. Hayes came back to the house to settle his grudge with Lovess and to see that no word got to town about what was going on. He could overtake the herd."

"So can we!" Talbot grunted. "Where you reckon Elenore is? She's the only one of that outfit I'd turn my hand to help. Hayes—well, all I want is to get that illegitimate lined up over my Winchester sights. I'm not so much with a six-shooter, but a Winchester, that's the lord's greatest leveler! Hayes ran a couple of sandies over me and made me take 'em. Now . . ."

Mechanically, Johnny glanced down at the trail where it branched to the Flying M. Ralph had turned that way. Dick Quell's horse tracks showed, heading for the Flagg. The posse forded the Vaca and came, late in the evening, up to the great Spear house. It was quiet as a graveyard.

Johnny yelled, but nobody answered. That seemed odd—as it had seemed queer in Mesita that Lovess had not sent one of the house servants instead of killing himself on the long, hard ride to town. But within the kitchen was what promised to be the answer to that small puzzle.

The wizened old boss cook, a Lovess retainer for twenty years, since trailherd days, lay sprawling before the range. He had been shot in the back. In a corner, face still twisted with fear, was his son and assistant. Talbot yelled from the yard beyond the main house that he had found a dead Mexican.

Within the house, they saw where Lovess had fallen and crawled with recovery of consciousness, out to the yard and the corral. The house was topsy-turvy. Lovess's desk had been smashed open. The old-fashioned iron safe in which he kept large sums of money had been blown open, and the explosion had increased the disorder of the long living room-office. Pictures had been blown from the wall.

Elenore's room was immaculate. Johnny, looking quickly to right and left inside it, was puzzled. A yell from outside, from High Pockets Sill, turned him back. A Spear cowboy had ridden up. He was gaping at the judge, who told him what had happened. At the end, he shook his head dumbly.

"When were you here last?" Johnny snapped.

"Yesterday. Hayes sent me hunting a horse over towards Bosque Verde. I chased the horse back and came home. I found him quicker'n Hayes figured I would. Miss Elenore—had she come back? She's been gone a week, you know. Visiting somewheres. She took Pete, that *vaquero* of hers."

"Perhaps, then, she wasn't here!" Biddle offered sympathetically. "That's doubtless the explanation, Johnny."

They rode out, taking the cowboy with them as posseman. Devoutly, Johnny hoped that Biddle was right. They met the Flying M party within five miles as they headed west toward the northern extremity of the Tortugas, not bothering to try cutting the trail of the stolen cattle and horses. Ralph rode with Mollison and three cowboys.

They continued west—and west. Presently, the moon rose. They came to the trail of the herd, which pointed vaguely southeast. It led straight toward the Flagg range of Orville Atchley. Even in the moonlight, it was plain to be seen.

Near midnight, they made camp. Johnny fell asleep but woke in darkness. A horse was coming. He sat up, as did the others. The horse stopped, fairly close at hand, as if the rider were staring at their fire. Then Dick Quell's voice sounded, calling Ralph Naile, which was the careful thing to do. He came on into the camp with Johnny's reassuring yell. He flung himself stiffly down and reached for food.

"Flagg is wiped out!" he said grimly. "Reckon Hayes took 'em by surprise. Atchley and a cowboy was lying outside the Flagg house, and I found the other cowboy, inside a mile—looked like he'd been riding for the house when they jumped him. Eight or nine of 'em. They just riddled him. Dollrags! Red dollrags . . ."

"It's time to take a chance!" Johnny said

abruptly, "And time to ride like hell. There's only one natural way to the Arroyo. We can shortcut and maybe come into that old owl hoot trail ahead of the herd. It's just a question of whether Hayes will keep to that old thieves' trail or blaze a new one. What do you think?"

"Better take a chance," Biddle counseled. "He's thinking of speed. He may have planned this long enough in advance to have plotted a trail we wouldn't think of. But that seems to be rather doubtful. I move that we try the shortcut."

They made coffee and ate again. It was three o'clock when Johnny led them off northeast. He blessed the days of his saddle tramping, in which he had learned this country in small and large. Without hesitation, he took them by stock trail and arroyo bottom, over hogbacks and around hills.

Dawn found them in rough country. But mid-morning brought them out of the little hills and down upon a wide greasewood flat. A mile and they began to cross deep rutted trails, but all were old, the ancient thieves' ways on the "owl hoot" trail.

"I'm satisfied we're ahead, now. I don't care how much they push the cattle, they're not going fast enough to be ahead," Johnny told the posse. "Now, I know a place to wait for 'em—Tinaja Rocks! They'll water there."

It was a queer jumble of red and black rocks,

with *tinajas*, spring-fed rock tanks, flowing out of caverns. They waited here and ate cold food—eighteen men. Johnny shook his head. No matter what quality of fighters Hayes had with him, and with the stolen stuff, they would find it hard to match these warriors around him.

Noon. From a pinnacle, the Spear cowboy on watch yelled that he sighted dust. Within two hours, they heard the thirsty cattle as they smelled water. Johnny, on a lower height of the rocks, saw how the big herd quickened gait. He studied it all through his glasses. Four men rode point, and as many more were on each wing. How many followed in the drag that the dust hid from him?

"They'll let 'em head for the water," he told his party, scrambling down recklessly, "and I don't think they'll be looking for us. Likely, they'll huddle up to water their horses. Judge, if I yell at 'em about once, to surrender, I reckon that'll serve the law, won't it?"

The little Kentuckian's eyes were shining. His mouth twitched under the white mustache. Then he put on a judicial expression and nodded silently.

CHAPTER 28

The herd broke. The point riders moved off to the side and let the cattle come. Johnny's party was lined up, now, behind the low breastworks of the end rocks, those that ran off to the right and left from the lofty central heights.

"Here they come!" Ralph called. "All in a huddle, like you said, Johnny. You'd think they were honest cowboys."

There were fully twenty riders, jogging along together. As Ralph had remarked, they came carelessly, talking loudly, like so many wage-earning riders. Whitey Kew was among them, Joe Downer, and hardcase men whom Johnny had known on the Heart, the D-Bar, and the Spear. He lifted himself when they were within thirty yards.

"It's all up!" he called to them. "We've got fifty men here. You might as well grab the stars!"

For ten seconds, perhaps, they gaped at him in stunned silence, pulling in their horses. Then Whitey Kew swore furiously. Either he or some-one near him, with Winchester out, jerked it up and opened fire. Down went Johnny as lead spattered against the rock on which he stood, and from his party came a rattle of fire that shredded the mass of men out in the open.

There were yelled oaths, and the cries of men

hit. Horses went down, kicking and squealing. Men raced off, low over the saddlehorns, in every direction but toward the rocks. Some flung themselves down behind clumps of greasewood and, from that small shelter, opened up on the posse. Then, out from the shelter of the high rocks, Johnny and a half dozen brought their horses. They charged out, shooting at the men behind the thin cover of the greasewood, following those who fled. The battle became a series of personal combats.

Johnny found himself alone, racing after Joe Downer. Not a man was in sight on either side of them. Downer, a hundred yards in the lead, suddenly whirled his horse, stopped him, and lifted his Winchester deliberately. Johnny pulled in his horse and snapped out two shots. Downer blazed away wildly then, but missed, as Johnny had missed. He began to run once more. He tried it twice, after that. Johnny closed up the distance between them. And Downer suddenly pulled in and lifted his hands.

"I'm out of shells!" he said sullenly. "You got me!"

"Where's Hayes?" Johnny yelled at him. "If he was with the herd, I couldn't see him. Where'd he go?"

Downer fished tobacco and papers from a pocket of his sweat-soaked shirt. He was a smallish man, dark of face, with cunning eyes.

Now he looked up from his cigarette at Johnny.

"You kind of like Elenore Lovess," he drawled. "Now don't you, Johnny? All right . . . suppose me and you make a trade. Suppose I tell you something you'd damned well like to know . . . Will you let me beat that necktie party at the Rocks?"

"I'll do this," Johnny said thickly. A great fear was in him; his hand shook on the saddlehorn. "If you tell me what I'm thinking, and tell me straight, and it helps, you can ride out of the country, and I'll let you go!"

"I believe you," Downer said, after a long, searching stare at him. "Hayes was going to catch up with us. Elenore, she was off visiting. Hayes aimed to waylay her as she came home and bring her along. He was tolerable drunk when he bragged to me and Whitey Kew about it. It was about Elenore that he fell out with Hugh Lovess, and he says that by the time she's been Queen of Hell Gate Arroyo a spell, she'll not be so standoffish."

"Where did he aim to waylay her?" Johnny gritted.

"Between Aden and Guadalupe Grande. Now you promised . . ."

"You're going with me! If it's like you say, you go free; if it's not—lord help you, Joe Downer. Come on!"

He waved the one-time D-Bar owner forward,

and Downer, after a long glance at Johnny's face, raked his horse, and they broke into a lope.

Johnny turned due north. He had that country between Aden and Guadalupe Grande pictured in his mind. But other pictures came: of Hayes riding out into the trail to catch Elenore's bridle reins; of Hayes grinning at the girl. He shook his head, but the pictures persisted. Downer yelled at him after a while. They would kill the horses. Johnny snarled at him and put hand to pistol.

He rode like a man in a nightmare, paying no attention to the country. At a guess, Elenore had been visiting the Cervantes girls. The great Cervantes ranch lay between Aden and Guadalupe Grande. Perhaps Hayes had known exactly where to wait for Elenore. He could only guess.

They passed Guadalupe Grande near dusk, leaving it off to the east of them. And here luck favored Johnny. He met a Mexican of the Cervantes riders. The *vaquero* had seen Elenore that morning, with Pedro, her bodyguard, leaving the Cervantes place. It was her second visit to the Cervantes girls within a week. Johnny thanked him swiftly and rode on. Joe Downer looked cunningly at Johnny. He began to beg to go.

"All right!" Johnny decided suddenly. "Straight north, though, Downer. That's the only safe direction for you!"

He came to the Cervantes's private road and rode through the dusk, staring for something that would tell him whether or not he was on the right track. Up the road crawled a queer thing, like a great beetle. Johnny approached carefully. He knew that it was a man, but why a man should crawl?

It was Pedro, the *vaquero*, who had been Elenore's bodyguard. He had been shot three times. It was a marvel that he lived, but he did more than merely survive—he crawled doggedly on, hunting for someone to hear his story.

"Near noon, Juancito!" he croaked. "Hayes came from behind a clump of brush on the road to Aden—it may be a mile, or it may be two miles, from here. I do not know how far I may have crawled. Me, he shot without warning. He laughed at the little one. He led her away westward."

There was little Johnny could do for Pedro, except to bandage him and give him water and whiskey in canteen and bottle. Then he rode on. It was two miles to the place where the blood and tracks in the dust told of the meeting. Within a hundred yards of the spot, Pedro's horse still grazed. Johnny shifted saddles. It was a good horse and fresh.

He followed the tracks as long as he could see them. After that, he could only trust that he went in the right direction. Would Hayes ride all night? That was the question.

He saw a far-off fire at last. He came cautiously

up to it and found that it was a sheep camp of Nacho Howze, one of the northernmost outposts of the half-breed sheep king's wide empire. The herder greeted Johnny cautiously, and hearing his name, he was more courteous, and he had a tale to tell. From a hilltop, he had seen Hayes and the girl. No more than four o'clock by the sun, it had been.

"There is the old log house on Good Water Creek," he suggested, when Johnny wondered aloud where Hayes would go. "I watched them over the last hill, Juancito. Straight toward Buen Agua they went. Perhaps the man knows of it and will sleep there."

Johnny flung him thanks and a month's pay: six silver dollars. He took directions for making Good Water Creek. He rode on, no more than five miles, so the herder said.

And there was one faint red line in a window when he neared the old cabin. He slid down from his horse. Mechanically, he looked to the hang of his six-shooter. Then he went toward the place, moving very quietly. He made the wall. A droning voice sounded, but the words were indistinguishable.

". . . just foolishness. You might as well take it sensible. I am not a man to take insults, and I have got what I went after every time. You might as well make up your mind to take it like she lays, then I'll untie you, and, later on, when it is convenient, we'll get married in the Arroyo. I . . ."

Johnny edged closer still, moving toward the corner. He made it and peered around. The doorway was open, doorless. Through it, firelight shone. And a shadow moved as the voice, Nathan Hayes's voice, grew irritable and threatening, "Either way, you're going to Hell Gate with me. Now, it can be nice and pleasant, like I told you, or it can be right hard. I'm easy going with women, but if you cross me, I ain't! And when I get you down to the Arroyo, all I have to do is lift my hands and say, 'I don't want her!'

"The whole bunch will start for you. You think about that, Elenore."

CHAPTER 29

Johnny lay stiffly, staring toward the pale orange rectangle that was the log cabin's door. There was still no answer from the girl. He wondered if she had been hurt; if she were unable to talk, and with that thought, red fury began to rise in Johnny Raff. It was like the moment when he looked down at Kesall's sneering dark face in the Congress, and recalled Edmund Friarson's murder.

It was a deeper fury. Impulsively, he moved to come to his feet and go charging into that door and blast Nathan Hayes with pistol fire, but he caught himself. He could take no chances here. There was Elenore to consider—she might be hit by stray lead, or Hayes might turn one of his deadly Colts upon her. Johnny knew the tall, dark man's vindictiveness; he was quite capable of killing Elenore to keep her from getting away.

He heard Hayes's voice again, higher, now, angrier, and now Elenore answered him. She called him a drunken rat. There followed the sharp sound of clapping hands. Johnny scowled uncertainly, then he knew that Hayes had struck her.

"That won't get you a thing!" the girl cried furiously, "any more than killing Pedro! You're swelled up because you were the Spear foreman for a while. You thought that men looked at you because you were Nate Hayes—but it wasn't! It was because you were foreman of the biggest outfit in the country. Now, you're due to learn some other things!"

Hayes laughed suddenly.

"And so are you, Sweetheart! So are you! Hell Gate Arroyo's going to be your little red schoolhouse, and Professor Hayes'll teach you plenty."

"You'll learn what it's like to stand on your own feet with Hugh Lovess coming at you, and others—like Johnny Raff!"

"Johnny Raff!" Hayes cried contemptuously and laughed again. "A damn kid that's played in hell's own luck and got all swelled up like a poisoned pup! One of these days, when I get things fixed the way I want 'em in Hell Gate, you know what I'm going to do? I'm going to get a bunch of good boys together and take 'em to Mesita, maybe to Aden, too! I'm going to pull up that place by the roots, wipe out the banks and run off everything worth taking from all the outfits, same as we cleaned the Spear this trip, and your little Johnny is going to dangle from a cottonwood."

Johnny shrugged. He had no plan, still. Perhaps he could work up close to the door, lean in, and cover or kill Nathan Hayes without endangering the girl. He got on his knees.

"Hugh Lovess will have you hanging from a cottonwood, long before that!" Eleanore told Hayes scornfully.

"Yeah?" Hayes said quickly. "Hugh Lovess is . . ."

Then he checked himself. Johnny thought that Hayes did not want to tell the girl that he had shot her father. Not tonight. He was squatting now, Johnny. He felt for his Colt. Then his head came instinctively around to face the dark line of brush on the creek's bank. It seemed to him that he had heard a small noise down there, louder than the murmur of water on stones, louder and nearer.

But he heard it no more, and presently he faced the cabin again, on his feet, crouching. After all, the night was full of sounds. That noise might have been no more than a hoof loosened rock dropping from the bank where Hayes and Elenore had crossed the water. It . . .

He jumped two yards sideways like a startled cat with the thud of feet behind him. He turned as he jumped, and he lifted his Colt. There was a dark blob streaking at him, and from the center of the moving figure came a spurt of yellowish flame. Johnny fired at it, fired again, then it was passing him and shooting. It was running for the cabin. He fired again and saw the figure jerk, fall, roll, and come up again.

"Nate!" Joe Downer screamed. "It's Raff! He shot me!"

There came from the cabin a hissing noise, and the fire light vanished. Hayes, evidently, had snatched up the water bucket or canteen and flung water upon the fire. Johnny ran toward the cabin after Downer. He flattened himself against the logs as Elenore screamed, "Johnny! For God's sake!"

Again, there was a sound of a hand upon her face. Then a mumbling, as if that hand clamped shut her mouth, and still she tried to scream her warning.

Johnny moved a little. There was a window and another door. They showed a little lighter than the darkness of the room, and in the door, he made out for an instant the vague shape of someone moving. He was afraid to shoot. It might be Hayes and Elenore together. He moved back from the door and worked toward the corner. From a window over him, then, came a shot.

The lead seemed fairly to scorch his cheek. He leaned backward and lifted his pistol to fire into the window. It was an automatic movement, hardly more than part of his leaning. He had the odd feeling that he had actually heard the slug strike the bone of his target's head.

He ran back toward the door. Someone had gone out—Downer or Hayes. One, he had certainly hit in the window. So, either the cabin was empty, or Elenore alone was there.

“Johnny!” the girl’s voice came despairingly from the cabin. “He’s outside . . .”

Johnny whirled back to face the corner. Dimly silhouetted there, now, was a man. Johnny sank to his heels and fired his last shot. All but blending with the roar of it was the shot from the other. In the tiny interval between that miss and the second shot from the corner, Johnny hurled himself at the cabin door. He was inside before the man, Hayes or Downer, fired again. Instinctively, he counted the three shots that followed.

There was no time to reload his pistol. He lifted it like a club, gripping the curved handle hard, but the shooting stopped, and Johnny’s ears rang so that he could not tell whether the man was creeping to the door or around the cabin.

He turned toward that window from which the shot had come. That man had a loaded pistol. He went quietly toward it, was bending with left hand out, when there was a rush of feet from the door he had just left, and he turned, flailing out instinctively with the long Colt barrel. It struck the other somewhere, but the shot that followed seared Johnny’s ribs. He did not know how badly he was hurt.

There was another shot, and flame burned him about the stomach. Then he had hold of an arm, and a steely hand caught his throat. He jerked and twisted, letting the empty pistol drop. They crashed into the wall, staggered away, and fell.

Johnny knew, then, that it was Nathan Hayes, for Joe Downer was not so tall as he, and this was a big man.

He was under Hayes, but he had broken that grip on his throat, and now as he rolled, he smashed his fist to Hayes's face. Hayes half-grunted, half-groaned and drove his own fist to Johnny's body. It was a heavy blow, and Johnny gasped. Hayes struck him again. Johnny's elbows seemed to lose their strength; his hands dropped, and the fingers opened.

Hayes moved, seeming to lift himself. His hand brushed Johnny's face, and Johnny, fighting the weakness that held him, twisted his head and caught Hayes's wrist between his teeth. He clamped his jaws desperately, and Hayes cried out and began to rain wild blows with his free hand. Johnny was not weak now, and the hammering fist grazed his hard head more often than it landed. He got a knee up and jammed it into Hayes's body. Hayes toppled, and they rolled, Johnny still holding his bulldog grip on Hayes's wrist.

Johnny flung out his hand to brace himself against the dirt floor. His fingers touched a face, and he withdrew them jerkily, slapped a pistol, closed upon it. Hayes's hand was at his throat, now. Johnny lifted the gun, cocked. He lunged with it, and when the muzzle was jammed against Hayes, he let the hammer fall. The bellow of it was muffled, but Hayes fell off him, and Johnny, panting as he let Hayes's wrist go, rolled a little to fire a second time.

He sagged on the floor, shaking, gasping. He heard Elenore calling to him through the darkness, but he could not answer for a while. He got to hands and knees, at last, and began to crawl toward her, mumbling. She screamed.

He stopped, drew a long breath, and called her name.

"Johnny!" she cried incredulously. "I—oh, I thought it was Hayes."

"It came near being Hayes," he said grimly.

Then he was in the corner where she lay. He fumbled with the turns of stiff manila lariat that bound her, but his fingers were too stiff, too shaky. He got out his stock knife with difficulty and cut her loose.

"Are you hurt, Johnny?" she asked him anxiously. "Hayes . . ."

"Not hurt. Hayes . . . It's all right, now! Can you walk—just to a horse? We want to leave here."

She leaned on him, and they staggered across the room and out the front door. Johnny felt steadier. He helped her around the cabin and to the horses staked behind. He saddled hers and clasped his hands for her foot.

"I'm all right, now," she said. "I can ride. Where's your horse?"

"Back there, by the creek. I'll let his go with his saddle—no! The money from the Spear safe's in his *alforjas* . . ."

"Money from the safe?" she said gaspingly. "You mean that he robbed the house? Then . . ."

"He robbed the house, and he shot your father. But don't worry! Hugh Lovess is all right now. He's in town, and the doctor says he'll be riding in six weeks. But I'll bring his horse and saddle with us."

Presently, sitting in his own saddle again, with Hayes's big bay following, Johnny led the girl across the creek and back over the trail by which he had come.

"There's one of Nacho Howze's herders four or five miles ahead," he told her. He had command of himself now, physically and mentally. "We'll use up the night with him and go on in the morning."

They made the camp of the sheep herder without talking. The herder made the Lady of the Spear and the famous Johnny Raff very welcome and fed them beans and mutton. At last, they were by the fire, the herder gone to a hilltop.

Elenore took Johnny's tobacco and papers and rolled him a cigarette. She lit it, drew in smoke, and blew it high over her head. "How did you find out about everything?" she asked him, leaning to give him the cigarette. "About me?"

He told her curtly, and when he was done, flipped the stub of the cigarette into the fire. The red gash on his ribs burned. His head ached. He moved and, with the chafe of shirt against wound, swore jerkily.

"Just a burn," he told her when she asked what it was. "You know, that man Hayes is just beyond me. When I was riding for the Spear, we got along well enough. I knew my work, and he knew I knew it. He never did more than tell me what to do. Then, all at once, it looked like he turned on me like a mad dog. It was like . . . Why, you might think that he'd started hating me! I don't know what happened; what he had in his mind . . ."

"You don't know?" she cried, leaning to stare at his face in the fire's light. "You said that once before. So, I suppose you don't. Oh, Johnny! You are a sharp boy, and a top hand in most ways, but some things are just too much for you. You're blind, as I've said before. Nate hated you because . . ."

She stopped, and Johnny turned a frowning face toward her.

"He wanted me. And he knew that he didn't have a chance of getting me, except as he got me today, for I had made up my mind about him, Johnny. There was a time when I thought that I did want him. He was big and swaggering and a handsome animal. You were just a nice boy, until you tied down your holsters on Friarson's account. After that . . ."

"Are you trying to tell me," Johnny said slowly, very carefully, "that Nate Hayes was jealous of me? If you are, what made him jealous? He knew that you didn't give a hoot in hell about me when I was on the Spear—"

". . . when you were on the Spear," she nodded. "But he made his move after you'd done what nobody in the High Mesa country thought you could do; after you'd opened up the war on Veck and Zagin and killed that Mexican rattlesnake, Tigre Lopez. I told him that I didn't want him; I told him more than that."

"I still don't see daylight," Johnny shrugged. "Every time I met you, you were full of good advice—patronizing! That was you. I couldn't do anything against the Martinez Monkeys. I'd better hightail it for Mexico. Maybe, someday, I could come back, and Hugh Lovess would be kind and condescending and give me my old job on the Spear. You stopped Hayes at the 77 when he was going to string me up, and you informed me that you'd have done the same for a Mex' sheep herder. You didn't care . . ."

"No? No? Then why did I ride hellbent for Aden when I found out that Hayes had bought Fierro and sent him with a fake message from me to put you in Vardaman's hands? Why did I camp there and bribe that rascally turnkey who sold me out to Martinez the next minute? I paid him three hundred good Spear dollars to open your cell door, Johnny Raff, and . . ."

"I'll be damned," Johnny marveled. "I will! In spite of the fact that I'm not big and swaggering and a handsome animal, you can find something about me . . ."

He twisted on the blanket, caught her hands, and drew her to him, shaking his head. He drew her arms up around his neck, held them there, and looked down at her. Her face lifted a little, and he bent to her eager mouth.

"Johnny, Johnny!" she said gaspingly, after a while, and pulled back a little, opening her eyes. "You're not big, and you really don't swagger, except in a Johnny Raff way, but you're a handsome enough animal to worry any woman. I'll bet you've had the girls in Bravo scratching each other's eyes out."

"Not all of 'em," Johnny grinned. "Probably not more than half of 'em. When did you first love me? I went to work for Hugh Lovess the day after I saw you first."

"It was that horrible day on the 77, when I rode up and saw you jerked off that horse—Ah, Johnny, the world went black. I knew that, without you, it would always be black."

She hid her face against his shirt and shuddered. Johnny patted her shoulder, put his lips to the slim, bowed neck.

"You know, I feel humble," he said in a low voice, "for it looked like ending up at the loop of a rope, or under somebody's lead, or at best, sliding across the river with the whole country shooting at me. And now . . ."

She lifted her head to stare at him and began to laugh.

"Humble! You? The trouble with us all, including Yours Always, was that we thought that, too, the whole High Mesa country. You'd always been so good-natured and sort of meek, and that reminds me—isn't there something, somewhere about the meek inheriting the earth? Well, that's your particular brand of meekness!"

"Ah, well," Johnny Raff said placidly, "if it's meekness, it's meekness, and it's a family property, now. So . . ."

He drew her to him and lifted her chin with a hand under it.

ABOUT THE AUTHOR

Born in Arkansas and brought up in Texas, Eugene Cunningham served in the US Navy, traveled the world, and returned to the U.S. in 1919 to become a writer. He sold his first story in 1920 and went on to publish more than 400 stories in the pulps. Cunningham was a prolific Western writer and even wrote some mystery and sea stories. He also penned more than twenty novels. His nonfiction title, *Triggernometry*, examines the gunfighters of the Wild West. His action-packed stories are filled with characters involved in an intricately plotted contest between good and evil, and he used the peak-and-valley technique of keeping the hero in constant trouble before the inexorable climax. Cunningham died at his home in San Francisco in 1957.

Center Point Large Print
600 Brooks Road / PO Box 1
Thorndike, ME 04986-0001 USA

(207) 568-3717

US & Canada:
1 800 929-9108
www.centerpointlargeprint.com